PENGUIN CLASSICS
A Crime in Holland

T0248712

'I love reading Simenon. He makes me think of Chekhov'
William Faulkner

'A truly wonderful writer . . . marvellously readable – lucid,
simple, absolutely in tune with the world he creates'
Muriel Spark

'Few writers have ever conveyed with such a sure touch the
bleakness of human life'
A. N. Wilson

'One of the greatest writers of the twentieth century . . .
Simenon was unequalled at making us look inside, though
the ability was masked by his brilliance at absorbing us
obsessively in his stories'
Guardian

'A novelist who entered his fictional world as if he were part
of it'
Peter Ackroyd

'The greatest of all, the most genuine novelist we have had in
literature'
André Gide

'Superb . . . The most addictive of writers . . . A unique teller
of tales'
Observer

'The mysteries of the human personality are revealed in all
their disconcerting complexity'
Anita Brookner

'A writer who, more than any other crime novelist, combined
a high literary reputation with popular appeal'
P. D. James

'A supreme writer . . . Unforgettable vividness'
Independent

'Compelling, remorseless, brilliant'
John Gray

'Extraordinary masterpieces of the twentieth century'
John Banville

GEORGES SIMENON

A Crime in Holland

Translated by SIÂN REYNOLDS

PENGUIN BOOKS

PENGUIN CLASSICS

Published by the Penguin Group
Penguin Books Ltd, 80 Strand, London WC2R ORL, England
Penguin Group (USA) Inc., 375 Hudson Street, New York, New York 10014, USA
Penguin Group (Canada), 90 Eglinton Avenue East, Suite 700, Toronto, Ontario, Canada M4P 2Y3
(a division of Pearson Penguin Canada Inc.)
Penguin Ireland, 25 St Stephen's Green, Dublin 2, Ireland (a division of Penguin Books Ltd)
Penguin Group (Australia), 707 Collins Street, Melbourne, Victoria 3008, Australia
(a division of Pearson Australia Group Pty Ltd)
Penguin Books India Pvt Ltd, 11 Community Centre, Panchsheel Park, New Delhi – 110 017, India
Penguin Group (NZ), 67 Apollo Drive, Rosedale, Auckland 0632, New Zealand
(a division of Pearson New Zealand Ltd)
Penguin Books (South Africa) (Pty) Ltd, Block D, Rosebank Office Park, 181 Jan Smuts Avenue,
Parktown North, Gauteng 2193, South Africa

Penguin Books Ltd, Registered Offices: 80 Strand, London WC2R ORL, England

www.penguin.com

First published in French as *Un Crime en Hollande* by Fayard 1931
This translation first published 2014

015

Copyright 1931 by Georges Simenon Limited
Translation © Siân Reynolds, 2014
GEORGES SIMENON ® Simenon.tm
MAIGRET ® Georges Simenon Limited
All rights reserved

The moral rights of the author and translator have been asserted

Typeset in Dante by Palimpsest Book Production Limited, Falkirk, Stirlingshire
Printed and bound in Great Britain by Clays Ltd, Elcograf S.p.A.

ISBN: 978-0-141-39349-0

www.greenpenguin.co.uk

Penguin Books is committed to a sustainable
future for our business, our readers and our planet.
This book is made from Forest Stewardship
Council™ certified paper.

MIX
Paper from
responsible sources
FSC FSC® C018179
www.fsc.org

1. The Girl with the Cow

When Detective Chief Inspector Maigret arrived in Delfzijl, one afternoon in May, he had only the sketchiest notions about the case taking him to this small town located in the northernmost corner of Holland.

A certain Jean Duclos, professor at the University of Nancy in eastern France, was on a lecture tour of the northern countries. At Delfzijl, he was the guest of a teacher at the Naval College, Conrad Popinga. But Popinga had been murdered, and while no one was formally charging the French professor, he was being requested not to leave the town and to remain answerable to the Dutch authorities.

And that was all, or almost. Jean Duclos had contacted the University of Nancy, which had asked Police Headquarters in Paris to send someone to Delfzijl to investigate.

The task had fallen to Maigret. It was more unofficial than official, and he had made it less official still by omitting to alert his Dutch colleagues on his arrival.

On the initiative of Jean Duclos, he had received a rather confused report, followed by a list of people more or less closely involved in the case.

This was the list which he consulted, shortly before arriving at Delfzijl station:

Conrad Popinga (the victim), aged 42, former long-haul captain, latterly a lecturer at the Delfzijl Naval College. Married. No children. Had spoken English and German fluently and French quite well.

Liesbeth Popinga, his wife, daughter of a high school headmaster in Amsterdam. A very cultured woman. Excellent knowledge of French.

Any Van Elst, Liesbeth Popinga's younger sister, visiting Delfzijl for a few weeks. Recently completed her doctorate in law. Aged 25. Understands French a little but speaks it badly.

The Wienands family: they live in the villa next door to the Popingas. Carl Wienands teaches mathematics at the Naval College. Wife and two children. No knowledge of French.

Beetje Liewens, aged 18, daughter of a farmer specializing in breeding pedigree cattle for export. Has stayed twice in Paris. Speaks perfect French.

Not very eloquent. Names that suggested nothing, at least to Maigret as he arrived from Paris, after spending a night and a half the following day on the train.

Delfzijl disconcerted him as soon as he reached it. At first light, he had travelled through the traditional Holland of tulips, and then through Amsterdam, which he already knew. The Drenthe, a heath-covered wasteland crisscrossed with canals, its horizons, stretching thirty kilometres into the distance, had surprised him.

Here was a landscape that had little in common with picture-postcard Holland, and was a hundred times more Nordic in character than he had imagined.

Just a little town: ten to fifteen streets at most, paved with handsome red bricks, laid down as regularly as tiles on a kitchen floor. Low-rise houses, also built of brick, and copiously decorated with woodwork, in bright cheerful colours.

It looked like a toy town. All the more so since around this toy town ran a dyke, encircling it completely. Some of the stretches of water within the dyke could be closed off when the sea ran high, by means of heavy gates like those of a lock.

Beyond lay the mouth of the Ems. The North Sea. A long strip of silver water. Cargo vessels unloading under the cranes on a quayside. Canals and an infinity of sailing vessels the size of barges and just as heavy, but built to withstand ocean swells.

The sun was shining. The station master wore a smart orange cap, with which he unaffectedly greeted the unknown traveller.

Opposite the station, a café. Maigret went inside and hardly dared sit down. Not only was it as highly polished as a bourgeois dining room, it had the same intimate feeling.

A single table, with all the daily papers set out on brass rods. The proprietor, who was drinking beer with two customers, stood up to welcome the newcomer.

'Do you speak French?' Maigret asked.

A negative gesture. Slight embarrassment.

'Can you give me a beer . . . *bier*?'

Once he was seated, he took the slip of paper from his pocket. The last name on the list was the one that his eyes lighted on. He showed it, pronouncing the name two or three times.

'Liewens.'

The three men began conferring together. Then one of them, a big fellow wearing a sailor's cap, got up and beckoned to Maigret to follow him. Since the inspector had no Dutch currency yet, and offered to pay with a hundred-franc note, he was told repeatedly:

'*Morgen! Morgen!*'

Tomorrow would do! He could just come back.

It was homely. There was something very simple, naive even, about it. Without a word, his guide led Maigret through the streets of the little town. On their left was a shed full of ancient anchors, rigging, chains, buoys and compasses, spilling out on to the pavement. Further along, a sail-maker was working in his doorway.

And the window of the confectioner's shop displayed a bewildering choice of chocolates and elaborate sweet-meats.

'No speak English?'

Maigret shook his head.

'*Deutsch?*'

Same reply, and the man resigned himself to silence. At the end of one street, they were already in the countryside: green fields, a canal in which floating logs from Scandinavia took up almost the whole width, ready to be hauled through Holland.

At some distance appeared a large roof of varnished tiles.

'Liewens . . . *Dag, mijnheer!*'

And Maigret went on, alone, after vainly trying to thank this man who, without knowing him from Adam, had walked with him for a quarter of an hour to do him a favour.

The sky was clear, the air of astonishing limpidity. The inspector walked past a timber yard where planks of oak, mahogany and teak were stacked in piles as tall as houses.

A boat was moored alongside. Some children were playing. Then came a kilometre with no outstanding features. Floating tree trunks covered the surface of the canal, all the way. White fences surrounded fields dotted with magnificent cows.

Another clash between reality and his preconceived ideas. The word 'farm' for Maigret conjured up a thatched roof, a dunghill, a bustle of barnyard fowls.

And he found himself facing a fine newly built structure, surrounded by a garden full of flowers. Moored in the canal in front of the house was an elegant mahogany skiff. And propped against the gate, a lady's bicycle, gleaming with nickel.

He looked in vain for a bell. He called, without getting any reply. A dog came and rubbed against his legs.

To the left of the house ran a long low building with regularly spaced windows but no curtains, which could have been an ordinary shed but for the quality of the materials and especially its bright fresh paintwork.

A sound of lowing came from that direction, and Maigret went on, round the flowerbeds, to find himself in front of a wide open door.

The building was a cowshed, but a cowshed as immaculate as a dwelling. Red brick everywhere, giving a warm, almost sumptuous luminosity to the atmosphere. Runnels for water to run off. A mechanical system for distributing feed to the mangers, and a pulley behind each stall, whose purpose

Maigret discovered only later: to lift up the tails of the cows during milking so that the milk wouldn't be contaminated.

The interior was in semi-darkness. The cattle were all outside, except for one cow lying on its side in the first stall.

And a girl in her late teens was approaching the visitor, speaking to him at first in Dutch.

'Mademoiselle Liewens?'

'Yes. You're French?'

As she spoke, she kept her eyes on the cow. She had an ironic smile which Maigret did not at first understand.

Here again, his preconceived ideas were turning out to be wrong. Beetje Liewens was wearing black rubber boots, which gave her the look of a stable-girl. Her green silk dress was almost entirely covered up by a white overall.

A rosy face, too rosy perhaps. A healthy, happy smile, but one lacking any subtlety. Large china-blue eyes. Red-gold hair.

She had to search to find her first words in French, which she spoke with a strong accent. But she quickly re-acquainted herself with the language.

'Did you want to speak to my father?'

'To you.'

She almost pouted.

'Excuse me, please. My father has gone to Groningen. He won't be back until later. The two farmhands are on the canal, unloading coal. The maidservant is out shopping. And this cow has picked this moment to start calving! We weren't expecting it. And I'm all on my own.'

She was leaning against a winch, which she had prepared in case the birth needed assistance. She was smiling broadly.

It was sunny outside. Her boots shone as if polished. She had plump pink hands with well-kept nails.

'It's about Conrad Popinga that I . . .'

But she gave a start. The cow had tried to stand up with a painful movement and had fallen back again.

'Look out! Can you give me a hand?'

She picked up the rubber gloves lying ready for duty.

And that was how Maigret began his investigation by helping bring a pure-bred Friesian calf into the world, in the company of a girl whose confident movements revealed her physical training.

Half an hour later, with the newborn calf already nuzzling its mother's udder, Maigret was stooping alongside Beetje, soaping his hands up to the elbow under a brass tap.

'Is it the first time you've done anything like this?' she asked with a smile.

'Yes, the first time . . .'

She was eighteen years old. When she took off her white overall, the silk dress moulded her generous curves, which, perhaps because of the sunny day, looked extremely fetching.

'We can talk over a cup of tea. Come into the house.'

The maidservant was back. The parlour was austere and rather dark, but spoke of refined comfort. The small panes in the windows were of a scarcely perceptible rose tint, which Maigret had never before encountered.

Shelves full of books. Many works on cattle breeding and veterinary science. On the walls hung farming diplomas and gold medals won at international exhibitions.

In the middle of all that, the latest publications by Claudel, André Gide and Paul Valéry . . .

Beetje's smile was flirtatious.

'Would you like to see my room?'

She was watching for his reaction. No bed, but a divan covered with a blue velvet spread. Walls papered with Jouy prints. Some dark-stained book shelves with more books and a doll bought in Paris, clad in a frou-frou dress.

One might almost have called it a boudoir, and yet there was a rather solid, serious and down-to-earth feel about it.

'Like a room in Paris, don't you think?'

'I'd like you to tell me what happened last week.'

Beetje's face clouded, but not over much, not enough to suggest that she was taking the events too tragically.

Otherwise, would she have given him that beaming smile of pride as she showed him her room?

'Let's go and have our tea.'

And they sat down facing each other, in front of a teapot covered with a sort of crinoline tea cosy to keep it warm.

Beetje had to search for the right words. She did more than that. She fetched a French dictionary, and sometimes broke off for quite a long time to find the exact word.

A boat with a large grey sail was gliding along the canal, propelled by a pole for want of wind. It manoeuvred its way through the tree trunks in mid-stream.

'You haven't been to the Popingas' house yet?'

'I arrived an hour ago, and all I've had time to do is help you to deliver the calf.'

'Yes . . . Conrad was so nice, a really lovely man . . . He

went all over the world as second lieutenant and then first
... Is that what you say in French? Then once he had his
master's certificate, he got married, and because of his
wife he took a job at the Naval College. That wasn't so
exciting. He used to have a little sailing boat too. But
Madame Popinga is afraid of the water. He had to sell it.
He just had a rowing boat on the canal after that. You saw
mine? Well, almost the same kind! In the evenings, he
tutored pupils. He worked very hard.'

'What was he like?'

At first she didn't understand the question. She ended
up going to fetch a photograph of a strapping, youngish
man, with cropped hair, rosy cheeks and light-coloured
eyes, who seemed to radiate bonhomie and good health.

'That's Conrad. You wouldn't think he was forty, would
you? His wife is older ... About forty-five. You haven't
seen her? And very different ... For instance, here everyone's Protestant of course ... I go to the Dutch Reformed
Church, which has more modern views. But Liesbeth Popinga goes to the Reformed Church of the Netherlands,
which is stricter ... more, what's the word? Conserving?'

'Conservative.'

'Yes. And she is the chairwoman of all the local charities ...'

'You don't like her?'

'Oh yes ... but it's not the same. She's the daughter of
a headmaster, you must understand. My father's just a
farmer ... But she's very nice, kind ...'

'What happened?'

'There are lots of lectures here ... It's just a small town, population five thousand. But people like to keep up with ideas. And last Thursday, Professor Duclos was here, from Nancy. You've heard of him?'

She was amazed that Maigret didn't know of the professor, whom she had assumed to be a national celebrity in France.

'He's a top lawyer. A specialist on crime, and what's the right word? Psychology of crime? He was giving this talk on the responsibility of criminals. That's right, is it? You must correct me if I make mistakes. Madame Popinga chairs the committee and the lecturers always stay at her house.

'At ten p.m. there was a small private party. Professor Duclos, Conrad Popinga and his wife. Wienands and his wife and children. And me . . . It was at the Popingas'. About a kilometre from here, it's on the Amsterdiep like this house. The Amsterdiep is the canal you can see. We had a glass of wine and some cakes. Conrad switched on the wireless. Oh yes, I nearly forgot, Any was there, Madame Popinga's sister, she's a lawyer too . . . Conrad wanted people to dance. They rolled back the carpet. The Wienands family left early because of the children. The little one was crying. They live next door to the Popingas. And at midnight, Any was feeling sleepy. I had my bike. Conrad saw me back home, he took his bike too.

'When I got back here, my father was waiting up for me. And it was only next day that we heard what had happened. All of Delfzijl was in an uproar.

'I don't think it was my fault. When Conrad got back home, he went to put his bike in the shed behind the house. And someone shot him with a revolver! He fell down, and in half an hour he was dead. Poor Conrad! With his mouth open.'

She wiped away a tear, which looked incongruous on that smooth cheek as pink as a rosy ripe apple.

'And that's all?'

'Yes. The police came from headquarters at Groningen to help the local gendarmes. They said the shot had been fired from inside the house. Apparently, the professor was seen right afterwards holding a revolver in his hand. And that was the gun that had been fired.'

'Professor Jean Duclos?'

'Yes! So they didn't let him leave.'

'So, in all, in the house at that time, there were just Madame Popinga, her sister Any and Professor Duclos?'

'Ja!'

'And that evening, the other people present were the Wienands family, yourself and Conrad . . .'

'And oh yes, there was Cor . . . I forgot.'

'Cor?'

'Short for Cornelius, a pupil at the Naval College. He was taking private lessons.'

'When did he leave?'

'The same time as Conrad and me. But he would have turned left on his bike, to get back to the college boat, which is moored on the Ems Canal. Do you take sugar?'

Steam rose from the teacups. A car had just stopped at the foot of the three steps up to the house. Shortly afterwards, a large burly man, grey-haired, with a serious expression, entered the room: his bulk emphasizing his calm presence.

This was Farmer Liewens, waiting for his daughter to introduce the visitor.

He shook Maigret's hand vigorously, but without saying anything.

'My father doesn't speak French.'

She served the farmer a cup of tea, which he drank standing up, with small sips. Then she told him about the calf's birth, speaking in Dutch.

She must also have mentioned the part played by the inspector in that event, since her father looked at him in astonishment tinged with irony, before, with a stiff bow, going off to the cowshed.

'So, is the professor in prison?' Maigret asked.

'No, he's at the Van Hasselt Hotel, with a gendarme attached to him.'

'And Conrad?'

'His body has been taken to Groningen . . . Thirty kilometres away. A big town with a university, population a hundred thousand. Where Jean Duclos had been welcomed the day before. It's all so dreadful, isn't it? Nobody can understand it.'

Dreadful, perhaps. But it was hard to feel that way! No doubt because of the clear air, the cosy, welcoming surroundings, the tea steaming on the table and the little town itself, looking like a toy village someone had set down by the seaside for fun.

By leaning out of the window one could see, looming over the brick houses, the smokestack and gangway of a large cargo vessel being unloaded. And the boats floating down the Ems towards the sea.

'Did Conrad usually accompany you home?'

'Every time I went to their house. He was a good friend.'

'And Madame Popinga didn't mind?'

Maigret made the remark almost at random, since his gaze had fallen on the young woman's tempting bosom, and perhaps because the sight of it had brought some warmth to his own cheeks.

'Why would she?'

'I don't know. Night time . . . the two of you . . .'

She laughed, showing healthy teeth.

'In Holland, it's always . . . Cor used to see me home too.'

'And *he* wasn't in love with you?'

She didn't say yes or no. She chuckled. A little chuckle of satisfied coquettishness.

Through the window, her father could be seen taking the calf out of the shed, carrying it like a baby and placing it on the grass in the field, in the sunlight.

The creature wobbled on its slender legs, almost fell to its knees, then suddenly tried to gallop for a few metres before stopping still.

'And Conrad never kissed you?'

Another laugh, accompanied by a very slight blush.

'Yes, he did.'

'And Cor?'

This time she was more formal, looking away for a moment.

'Yes, he did too, but why do you ask?'

She looked at him oddly. Perhaps she was expecting Maigret to kiss her as well.

Her father was calling from outside. She opened the window. He spoke to her in Dutch. When she turned back, it was to say:

'Excuse me, please. I have to go to town to find the mayor, about the calf's pedigree. It's very important. You're not going to Delfzijl too?'

He went out with her. She took the handlebars of her nickel-plated bicycle and walked alongside him, swinging her hips, already those of a mature woman.

'It's so beautiful here, isn't it? Poor Conrad! He will never see it again. The swimming opens tomorrow. He used to come every day, other years. He'd stay in the water for an hour.'

Maigret, as he walked, kept his eyes on the ground.

2. The Baes's Cap

Contrary to his usual habit, Maigret noted down a few physical details, mainly topographical, and that was in fact a true case of intuition, since, in the end, the solution proved to be a matter of minutes and metres.

Between the Liewens farm and the Popinga residence, the distance was about twelve hundred metres. Both buildings were on the bank of the canal, and to go from one to the other, the only route was the towpath.

This canal had more or less fallen into disuse, following the construction of a much wider and deeper channel, the Ems Canal, linking Delfzijl to Groningen.

The smaller canal, the Amsterdiep, silted up, meandering and shaded by fine trees, was now used almost exclusively for floating timber, and by the occasional boat of low tonnage.

A few farms scattered about. A boatyard for repairs.

On leaving the Popinga house to go to the farm, the next building one reached, just thirty metres away, was the Wienands villa. Then came a plot under construction. After that, a long empty stretch, and the timber yard with its stacks of wood.

Beyond the yard came another uninhabited section, preceded by a bend in the canal and the path. From there, the Popinga windows were clearly visible, as was, just to the left, the white-painted lighthouse on the far side of the town.

'Does the lighthouse have a revolving beam?' Maigret asked.

'Yes.'

'So at night, it must light up this part of the road . . .'

'Yes,' she exclaimed again, with a little laugh, as if it brought back some happy memory.

'Not too good for courting couples!' he concluded.

She left him before they reached the Popinga house, claiming that she could take a short cut, but probably so as not to be seen in his company.

Maigret did not stop. The house was modern, brick-built, with a small garden in front, a vegetable plot behind, a path along the right-hand side, and a patch of waste ground on the left.

He preferred to head for the town, only five hundred metres further along. His steps took him to the lock separating the canal from the harbour. The basin was crammed with boats of between a hundred and three hundred tons, moored side by side, masts in the air, forming a floating world.

On the left was the Van Hasselt Hotel, into which he walked.

A dark lounge with varnished woodwork, and a complex smell of beer, genever and furniture polish. A large billiard table. Another table with newspapers stretched on brass rods.

A man sitting in the corner stood up as soon as Maigret arrived and came to meet him.

'Are you the man the French police have sent me?'

He was tall and gaunt, with a long face, sharp features, horn-rimmed glasses and a crew cut.

'You must be Professor Duclos,' Maigret replied.

He hadn't expected him to look so young. Duclos was about thirty-five to thirty-eight. But there was something slightly unusual about him that struck Maigret.

'You're from Nancy?'

'I have the chair of sociology in the university there.'

'But you weren't born in France?'

It was as if a little tussle had started.

'I was born in French Switzerland. But I've been naturalized a French citizen. I completed all my studies in Paris and Montpellier.'

'And you're a Protestant?'

'How can you tell?'

By nothing and everything! Duclos belonged to a category of men that the inspector knew well. Men of science. Study for study's sake. Ideas for ideas. A certain austerity of manner and lifestyle, combined with a taste for international contacts. A passion for lectures, conferences and exchanges of letters with foreign correspondents.

He seemed rather on edge, if this could be said of a man whose expression never changed. On his table stood a bottle of mineral water, together with two fat books and a sheaf of papers.

'I don't see the policeman who's supposed to be keeping you under observation.'

'I gave my word of honour I wouldn't leave here. Although, I have to tell you, I'm expected by literary and scientific

17

gatherings in Emden, Hamburg and Bremen. I was due to give my lecture in those three towns, before . . .'

A large blonde woman, the hotel proprietress, appeared and Jean Duclos explained to her in Dutch who the visitor was.

'I just took a chance in asking for a French policeman to be sent here. In fact, I am hoping to be able to shed light on this mystery myself.'

'Can you tell me what you know?'

And Maigret slumped into a chair before ordering:

'A Bols . . . in a big glass.'

'Here are some diagrams, done exactly to scale. I can give you a copy. The first is the ground floor of the Popinga house. With the corridor on the left, the parlour and dining room on the right. The kitchen at the back, and behind it a shed where Popinga kept his boat and the bicycles.'

'Were you all in the parlour?'

'Yes. Madame Popinga and Any went twice into the kitchen to make tea, because the housemaid had gone to bed. And here's the first floor: at the back, over the kitchen, is a bathroom; at the front of the house there are two rooms: on the left, the Popingas' bedroom; on the right a study, where Any slept on a divan. And at the back was the bedroom they had given me.'

'Which rooms could the shot have been fired from?'

'My bedroom, the bathroom and the dining room downstairs.'

'So tell me about the evening.'

'My lecture was a triumph. I gave it in the hall you can see there.'

A long room, decorated with paper chains, and evidently used for dances, banquets and dramatic productions. A stage with scenery representing the grounds of a chateau.

'Then we went to the Amsterdiep.'

'Along the canal bank? Can you tell me what order you went in?'

'I went ahead with Madame Popinga, who is a highly educated woman. Conrad Popinga was flirting with that silly little girl from the farm, who can only giggle and hadn't understood a word of my talk. Then there were the Wienands, and Any, and some pupil of Popinga's, an anaemic-looking boy.'

'You arrived at the house . . .'

'They will have told you that my lecture was about the responsibility of murderers. Madame Popinga's sister, Any, who has finished her law degree and will start teaching in the autumn, asked me for some details. We were led to discuss the role of the lawyer in criminal cases. Then we talked about forensics, and I remember I suggested she read some books by Professor Grosz of Vienna. I maintained that to commit a crime with impunity is virtually impossible. I talked about fingerprints, the analysis of all kinds of material traces and calculations . . . But Conrad Popinga kept pressing me to listen to Radio-Paris!'

Maigret showed only the shadow of a smile.

'And he succeeded. They were playing some jazz. Popinga went to fetch a bottle of cognac, and was amazed to find a Frenchman who didn't drink it. He took some himself, and so did the girl from the farm . . . They were very merry . . . They started dancing. "Just like in Paris!" Popinga was shouting.'

'You didn't like him!' Maigret remarked.

'An uncouth fellow, of no interest! Wienands, although he is mostly concerned with mathematics, was listening to us. A baby started to cry. The Wienands left. The farmer's daughter was in high spirits. Conrad offered to see her home, and they both went off on their bicycles. Madame Popinga showed me to my room. I sorted out some papers from my briefcase. I was just going to take notes for a book I'm writing when I heard a gunshot, from so close by that it could almost have been fired in my room. I rushed outside. The bathroom door was ajar. I pushed it. The window was wide open. And someone was groaning in the garden, near the bicycle shed.'

'Was the light on in the bathroom?'

'No. I leaned out of the window. And my hand touched the butt of a revolver, which I automatically picked up . . . I thought I saw someone lying on the ground near the shed. I made to go downstairs. And I bumped into Madame Popinga, who was coming out of her room, in shock. We both ran downstairs. We had got as far as the kitchen when we were joined by Any, who was so alarmed that she had come down in nothing but her petticoat. You'll see what I mean when you meet her.'

'And Popinga?'

'Half-dead. He looked up at us with great agonized eyes, clutching at his chest with one hand. At the moment I tried to lift him up, he stiffened. He was dead, a bullet through the heart.'

'And that's all you know?'

'We telephoned the gendarmerie, and the doctor. We called Wienands out, and he came to help us . . . I sensed a certain awkwardness around me. I'd forgotten that I had been seen holding the revolver. The gendarmes reminded me of this and asked me to explain. Then they requested me politely to remain available for further questioning.'

'And that was six days ago.'

'Yes. I've been working on the problem, trying to resolve it, because it *is* a problem. See these papers?'

Maigret tapped out his pipe, without looking at the papers in question.

'And you haven't left the hotel?'

'I could do, but I prefer to avoid any incidents. Popinga was very popular with his pupils and you meet them all the time around town.'

'And no physical clue has been found.'

'Ah yes, sorry. Any, who is carrying out her own investigation and hoping to identify the killer too, although she doesn't go about it methodically, sometimes brings me some more information. You ought to know that the bath in the Popinga bathroom is covered with a wooden lid, which converts it into an ironing board. The day after the murder, they took the lid off and found a shabby seaman's cap, which had never been seen in the house before. On the ground floor, a police search found the end of a cigar on the dining room carpet, very dark tobacco, Manila I think, such as none of them smoked, Popinga, Wienands or the young pupil. And I never smoke. And yet the dining room had been swept after dinner.'

'From which you deduce . . .'

'Nothing,' said Jean Duclos. 'I'll draw my conclusions in my own good time. I apologize for bringing you all the way here. And they could have picked a policeman who knew the language. You can be useful to me only in the event that they take any measures regarding me, in which case you would have to make an official protest.'

Maigret stroked his nose, while smiling a truly delicious smile.

'Are you married, Monsieur Duclos?'

'No.'

'And before this you were not acquainted with the Popingas, or the little sister Any, or any of the other people present?'

'No, none of them. They knew me, by reputation . . .'

'Naturally! Of course!'

And Maigret picked up the two carefully plotted diagrams, stuffed them in his pocket, touched his hat and went out.

The police station was modern, well-lit and comfortable. Maigret was expected. The station master had reported his arrival and they were astonished not to have seen him yet.

He went in as if to his own office, took off his light spring overcoat and placed his hat on a chair.

The inspector who had been sent from Groningen spoke French slowly and rather pedantically. A tall, blond, clean-cut young man, of remarkably affable manner, he underlined every sentence with a little nod, which seemed to indicate: 'You get my meaning? We are agreed on this?'

Although in truth Maigret hardly gave him time to start speaking.

'Since you've been on this case for six days,' he said, 'you must have checked the times.'

'What times?'

'It would be interesting for instance to know exactly how many minutes the victim took to escort Mademoiselle Beetje home, and then return. Wait! I'd also like to know what time Mademoiselle Beetje actually set foot back in the farm, where her father was waiting up for her, and he ought to be able to tell you that. And lastly, the time that young Cor arrived back at the college boat, where there is no doubt a night watchman.'

The Dutch inspector looked annoyed, stood up suddenly as if struck by inspiration, went towards the back of the room, and returned carrying a very shabby seaman's cap. Then, enunciating his words with exaggerated slowness, he said:

'We have found the owner of this item which was discovered in the bath . . . He is . . . He is a man we call "the Baes". In French you'd say "le patron", the boss.'

Was Maigret even listening?

'We have not arrested him, because we wish to keep him under observation, and he is popular in the district. You know the mouth of the Ems? When you reach the North Sea, about ten sea miles from here, you come to some sandy islands, which can be more or less completely submerged in the high equinoctial tides. One of these islands is called Workum. This man has settled there with his family and some farmhands, and taken it into his head to raise livestock. That's "the Baes" for you. He's been granted a state subsidy, because he has established squatter's rights. And he has even been appointed mayor of Workum, of which he is the only Dutch citizen. He has a motor launch, and comes and goes between his island and Delfzijl.'

Maigret still did not budge. The Dutchman winked.

'An odd fellow! Sixty years old, and as solid as a rock. He has three sons, all pirates like himself. Because . . . Listen! This is not the sort of thing to shout out loud. You know that Delfzijl is a port for handling timber from Finland and Riga . . . The steamboats that bring the logs here have part of the cargo on deck, held down with chains. But in emergencies, the captains have orders to cut the chains and jettison the deck cargo into the sea, to save the boat. You still don't see what I am driving at?'

And certainly Maigret gave no sign of being at all interested in this story.

'The Baes is a cunning man. He knows all the sea captains who come in here. He has his little arrangements with them. So when they are in sight of the islands, there's always a reason to be found for cutting at least one chain. Then several tons of timber go into the sea and the tide throws them up on Workum sands. Wreckers' rights. Now do you understand? And the Baes shares the proceeds with the captains. And it was *his* cap that they found in the bath. Just one problem. He only smokes a pipe. But he may not have been alone.'

'And that's it?'

'No. Ah no! Monsieur Popinga, who has contacts everywhere, or rather who *had*, was appointed Finnish vice-consul in Delfzijl a couple of weeks ago.'

The skinny young man was triumphant now, puffing with satisfaction.

'And where was the Baes's boat on the night of the crime?'

This time it was almost a shout.

'In Delfzijl. Moored at the quayside. Near the lock! In other words, fifty metres from the Popinga house.'

Maigret tamped more tobacco into his pipe, and paced up and down in the office, looking with a jaundiced eye at the reports, of which he could understand not a damned word.

'And you haven't anything else to go on,' he said suddenly, thrusting both hands into his pockets.

He was hardly surprised to see the other policeman blush.

'You know already?'

He checked himself.

'Of course, you have spent all afternoon in Delfzijl . . . French tactics.'

He seemed hesitant.

'I don't know yet what this statement means. It was on the fourth day. Madame Popinga turned up. She told me that she had consulted the minister, to see whether she ought to say anything. You know the layout of the house? Not yet? I can show you a diagram?'

'Thanks! But I've got one,' said Maigret, taking it from his pocket.

The other man, looking startled, went on:

'You see the Popingas' bedroom? From the window, you can glimpse only a little section of the road leading to the farm. Just the stretch that is lit up by the lighthouse every fifteen seconds.'

'And Madame Popinga was jealous, so she was spying on her husband?'

'She was looking out. She saw the two bikes on the way to the farm. Then her husband cycling back. Then about a hundred metres behind him, Beetje Liewens's bicycle.'

'In other words, after Conrad Popinga saw her home, Beetje returned on her own towards the Popinga house. So what does she say about this?'

'Who?'

'The girl.'

'Nothing so far. I didn't want to question her right away. It's very serious, and you may have chosen the right word. Jealousy. You understand? Monsieur Liewens is a member of the Council.'

'What time did Cor get back to the Naval College?'

'That we do know, five minutes past midnight.'

'And the shot was fired . . . ?'

'Five minutes before midnight . . . But there's the cap and the cigar . . .'

'And he has a bike?'

'Yes. Everybody cycles everywhere here. It's practical. I do it myself . . . But that night, he didn't have his bike with him.'

'The revolver has been examined?'

'Ja! It's Conrad Popinga's own gun. His service revolver. It was always loaded with six bullets, and inside a drawer of his bedside table.'

'And the shot was fired from how many metres away?'

26

'About six. The distance from the bathroom window. And also the distance from Monsieur Duclos's bedroom. And perhaps the shot wasn't fired from up above. We don't know, because Popinga, who was putting his bike away, could have been bending down. But there's the cap. And the cigar. Don't forget.'

'Cigar, phooey,' muttered Maigret to himself.

And out loud:

'Is Mademoiselle Any aware of her sister's statement?'

'Yes.'

'And what does she say about it?'

'She hasn't said anything. She's highly educated. She doesn't talk much. She's not like other girls.'

'Is she ugly?'

Every one of Maigret's interruptions had the knack of disconcerting the Dutch policeman.

'Well . . . not pretty.'

'Very well, she's ugly. And you were saying that . . .'

'She wants to find the murderer. She's working on it. She has asked to see the reports.'

Chance took a hand. A young woman came in, with a leather briefcase under her arm: she was dressed austerely, almost to the point of eccentricity.

She marched straight up to the Groningen police officer. She began speaking volubly in her own language, either not seeing the stranger, or taking no notice of him.

The Dutchman reddened, shifted from one foot to the other, shuffling his papers to give himself an air of authority and indicating Maigret with his eyes. But she did not deign to pay any attention to the Frenchman.

In despair, the Dutch inspector spoke in French, as if with regret.

'She says the law forbids you to question anyone on Dutch territory.'

'This is Mademoiselle Any?'

Irregular features. If not for the large mouth and uneven teeth, she wouldn't have been worse-looking than average. Flat-chested. Large feet. But above all, the forbidding self-confidence of the suffragette.

'Yes. According to the statutes, she's right. But I've told her that in practice . . .'

'Mademoiselle Any understands French, I believe?'

'I think so.'

The young woman didn't react, but waited, chin held high, for the end of this consultation between the two men, which did not appear to concern her.

'Mademoiselle,' said Maigret, with exaggerated gallantry, 'please accept my respects. Detective Chief Inspector Maigret, from Police Headquarters in Paris. All I wanted to know is what you thought about Mademoiselle Beetje and her relationship with Cornelius.'

She tried to smile. A shy, forced smile. She looked from Maigret to her compatriot and stammered in poor French:

'I not . . . I not understand very well.'

And the effort was enough to make her blush scarlet to the tips of her ears, while everything in her expression pleaded for release.

3. The Quayside Rats Club

There were about a dozen of them, all men, wearing heavy blue woollen jackets, seaman's caps and varnished clogs, some lounging against the town gates, others leaning their elbows on bollards, others again just standing around, their wide trousers making their legs look monumental.

They were smoking, chewing tobacco, spitting a lot, and now and then something made them all burst out laughing, slapping their thighs.

Four metres away from them floated the boats. Beyond lay the smug little town, surrounded by its dykes. Further along, a crane was unloading a collier.

At first the men did not notice Maigret strolling along the wharf. So he had plenty of time to observe them.

He had learned that in Delfzijl this group was known ironically as 'the Quayside Rats Club'. Without even being told, he could have guessed that most of these sailors spent the greater part of their days on the same spot, rain or shine, chatting lazily and sending jets of saliva to the ground.

One of them was the owner of three clippers, handsome vessels of four hundred tons equipped with sails and engines, one of which was just moving up the Ems and would soon be in port.

Other men seemed less distinguished; a ship's caulker

who probably didn't do much caulking and the keeper of a disused lock, still wearing his government service cap.

But in the middle of the group, one figure eclipsed all the rest, not only because he was the most massively built and the reddest of face, but because one sensed in him a man of stronger character.

Clogs, a jacket. And on his head a brand-new cap, which had not yet had time to mould itself to the shape of his skull, and consequently looked faintly ridiculous.

This was Oosting, commonly known as the Baes, smoking a short clay pipe as he listened to his neighbours talking.

A vague smile played on his face. From time to time, he removed the pipe from his mouth to allow the smoke to flow gently from his lips.

He reminded Maigret of a small-scale rhinoceros. A heavily built brute, but with mild eyes and something at the same time tough and gentle about his whole person.

His eyes were fixed on a boat about fifteen metres long, moored to the quayside. A swift boat with clean lines, probably a former yacht, though now dirty and cluttered.

This belonged to him, and from here it was possible to see the Ems estuary, twenty kilometres wide, and the distant glimmer of the North Sea: out there somewhere lay a golden brown sandbank known as the island of Workum, Oosting's domain.

Night was falling: the crimson rays of the setting sun painted the brick-built town even redder and glinted in fiery flashes on the scarlet lead paint of a cargo vessel undergoing repairs, reflected in the water of the harbour.

The Baes's gaze, as it wandered calmly across the scene,

contrived to take in Maigret as part of the landscape. His blue-green eyes were very small. They remained focused on the French inspector for a short while, after which the man tapped out his pipe against his wooden clog, spat, felt in his pockets for the pig's bladder he used to hold his tobacco, and settled himself more comfortably up against the wall.

From that point on, Maigret felt that gaze resting continuously on him, conveying neither bravado nor distrust: a cool and yet concerned gaze, one that was weighing up, appreciating and calculating.

Maigret had been the first to leave the police station, having arranged a later meeting with the Dutch inspector, whose name was Pijpekamp.

Any had remained inside, and presently went past, clutching her briefcase under her arm, leaning forward slightly, like a woman with no interest in anything happening in the street.

It wasn't Any that Maigret was watching, but the Baes, who followed her for a while with his eyes, then, with a more puckered brow, turned towards Maigret.

So, without really knowing why, Maigret moved towards the group, which fell silent. Ten faces turned in his direction, expressing a degree of surprise.

He addressed Oosting:

'Excuse me. Do you understand French?'

The Baes did not budge, appearing to be thinking. A lanky seaman standing alongside him explained in English and Dutch:

'Frenchman! Frans politie.'

The next minute was perhaps one of the strangest in Maigret's career.

The man he had spoken to, turning briefly towards his boat, seemed to hesitate.

It was clear that he wanted to ask the inspector to come aboard with him. One could see a small oak-panelled cabin, with its swinging lamp, a compass.

The other men waited. He opened his mouth.

Then suddenly he shrugged his shoulders, as if deciding: 'No, that's ridiculous!'

But that wasn't what he said. In a hoarse voice issuing from his throat, he uttered: 'No understand. *Hollands . . . English . . .*'

They could still see Any's dark silhouette, with her crepe mourning veil, crossing the bridge over the canal before taking the towpath along the Amsterdiep.

The Baes intercepted Maigret's glance at his new cap, but did not flinch. Rather, the shadow of a smile crossed his lips.

At that moment, the inspector would have given good money to be able to have a chat with this man in his own language, even for five minutes. His goodwill was such that he stammered out a few sentences in English, but his accent was so strong that nobody understood.

'No understand. Nobody understand!' repeated the man who had spoken.

So they resumed their conversation, while Maigret walked away with the vague feeling that he had been very close to the heart of the enigma and that now, for want of mutual comprehension, he was getting further away from it.

He turned round a few minutes later. The Quayside Rats were still chatting as the sun set, and its last rays cast a rosier glow over the heavy-jowled face of the Baes, still turned in Maigret's direction.

Until then, Maigret had in some sense been circling round the drama, saving until last the visit, always a painful one, to the house of mourning.

He rang the doorbell. It was just after six. He hadn't realized that this was the time when Dutch people eat their evening meal, and when a young housemaid opened the door, he could see in the dining room the two women sitting at the table.

They both stood up in a simultaneous movement with the slightly stiff air of well-brought-up schoolgirls.

They were dressed in black. The table was laid with teacups, wafer-thin slices of bread and cold meats. Despite the gathering dusk, the lamp was not lit but a gas-fired stove, its flames visible through its mica panes, was struggling against the dark.

It was Any who immediately thought to switch on the electric light, while the maid closed the curtains.

'Please forgive me,' said Maigret. 'I'm so sorry to disturb you at supper time.' Madame Popinga vaguely gestured towards an armchair and looked around her distractedly, while her sister retreated as far as possible into the room.

A similar atmosphere to the farm. Some modern furniture, but very conservatively modern. Muted colours combining in an elegant but gloomy harmony.

'You've come to . . .'

Madame Popinga's lower lip trembled, and she had to put her handkerchief to her mouth to stifle a sob that had suddenly broken out. Any didn't move.

'Forgive me. I'll come back . . .'

Madame Popinga shook her head. She was struggling to regain her composure. She must have been a good few years older than her sister. A tall woman, much more feminine. Regular features, a hint of broken veins in the cheeks, the odd grey hair.

And a modest dignity in every gesture. Maigret recalled that she was the daughter of a headmaster, spoke several languages and was well educated. But that didn't affect her timidity, the timidity of a respectable woman in a small town, liable to take fright at the slightest thing.

He also remembered that she belonged to the most austere of Protestant sects, and that she presided over all the Delfzijl charities and hosted the women's literary circles.

She regained her self-control. She looked at her sister as if asking for help.

'I'm sorry! But it's just so unbelievable, isn't it? Conrad! A man everyone loved.'

Her gaze fell on the wireless loudspeaker, standing in a corner, and she almost burst into tears.

'That was his only distraction,' she stammered. 'And his little boat on the Amsterdiep, on summer evenings. He worked so hard. Who could have done this?'

And as Maigret said nothing, she added, turning a little pink, in the tone she might have used if someone had argued with her:

'I'm not accusing anyone. I don't know. I just can't believe it, do you understand? The police thought of Professor Duclos, because he came out holding the revolver. But I don't know what happened. It's too horrible! Someone killed Conrad. But why? Why him? It wasn't even a burglary. So . . .'

'And you told the police what you saw from the window?'

She blushed deeper. Standing upright, one hand leaning on the dinner-table, she said:

'I didn't know if I should . . . I don't think Beetje did anything. It was just that by chance I saw. They told me the smallest little detail might help their enquiries. I asked the minister for advice. He told me to speak up. Beetje's a perfectly nice girl. Really, I don't see who . . . Somebody who should be in a lunatic asylum!'

She had no need to search for the right words. Her French was perfect, pronounced with a very slight accent.

'Any told me you've come from Paris. Because of Conrad! Are we to believe that?'

She had calmed down. Her sister, still standing in a corner of the room hadn't stirred, and Maigret could only partly see her, by way of a mirror.

'You'll need to look over the house, I assume?'

She was resigned to it. But she sighed:

'Could you go with . . . Any?'

A black dress moved in front of the inspector. He followed it up a staircase fitted with brand-new carpeting. The Popinga home, no more than ten years old, was built like a doll's house, with lightweight materials, hollow bricks and pine boards. But the paint which had been applied to all the woodwork gave it a fresh and bright look.

The bathroom door was the first to be opened. There was a wooden lid over the bath, transforming it into an ironing board. Maigret leaned out of the window, and saw the bicycle shed, the well-kept kitchen garden, and across the fields the town of Delfzijl, few of whose houses had two storeys, and none three.

Any was waiting at the door.

'I hear you're carrying out your own investigation,' Maigret said.

She shuddered, but didn't answer, and hurried to open the door of Professor Duclos's room.

A brass bedstead. A pitch-pine wardrobe. Lino on the floor.

'And this is whose bedroom?'

She had to make an effort to speak French.

'Of me . . . When I am here.'

'And you've often stayed here?'

'Yes . . . I . . .'

She was really very shy. The words stuck in her throat. Her eyes looked around for help.

'So since the professor was a guest here, you slept in your brother-in-law's study?'

She nodded yes and opened the door. A table laden with books, including new publications on gyroscopic compasses and on radio communication with ships. Some sextants. On the walls, photos of Conrad Popinga in the Far East and Africa in his uniform as first lieutenant or captain.

There was a display of Malayan weapons. Japanese enamels. On trestles lay some precision tools and a ship's compass in pieces, which Popinga must have been repairing.

A divan covered with a blue bedspread.

'And your sister's room?'

'Here, next door.'

The study communicated both with the professor's room and the Popingas' bedroom, which was furnished more stylishly. An alabaster lamp over the bed. A rather fine Persian carpet. Wooden colonial furniture.

'And you were in the study,' said Maigret thoughtfully.

A nod, yes.

'So you couldn't come out without going either through the professor's room or your sister's?'

Another nod.

'And the professor was in his room. And your sister in hers.'

She opened her eyes wide, her jaw dropped as if she'd had a terrible shock.

'And, you think . . . ?'

Maigret muttered as he paced through the three rooms:

'I don't think anything. I'm searching. I'm eliminating possibilities! And up to now, you are the only one who can logically be eliminated, unless we assume some complicity between you and either Duclos or Madame Popinga.'

'You . . . you . . .'

But he was carrying on talking to himself.

'Duclos might have fired the shot either from his room or the bathroom, that's clear. Madame Popinga could have gone into the bathroom. But the professor, who went in there immediately after hearing the shot, didn't see her. On the contrary, he saw her coming out of her room only a few seconds later.'

Perhaps she was now emerging a little from her shell. The student was taking over from the timid girl, as if inspired by this technical hypothesis.

'Maybe, someone shot from downstairs?' she said, her gaze now more focused and her thin body alert. 'The doctor says . . .'

'True, but that doesn't alter the fact that the revolver that killed your brother-in-law was certainly the one Duclos was holding. Unless the murderer threw the gun upstairs through the window.'

'Why not?'

'Obviously. Why not?'

And he went down the stairs, which seemed too narrow for him, the steps creaking under his bulk.

He found Madame Popinga standing in the dining room, apparently on the spot where he had left her. Any followed him in.

'Did Cornelius come here often?'

'Almost every day. He only had lessons three times a week, Tuesdays, Thursdays and Saturdays. But he came on the other days. His parents are in the East Indies. A month ago, he was told that his mother had died. She was dead and buried by the time he got the letter. So . . .'

'What about Beetje Liewens?'

There was a slightly awkward silence. Madame Popinga looked at Any. Any looked down.

'She used to come . . .'

'Often?'

'Yes.'

'Did you invite her?'

His questions were getting brusquer, more pointed. Maigret had the feeling he was making progress, if not in discovering the truth, at least in his penetration of the life in this house.

'No . . . yes.'

'She's a different kind of person from you and Mademoiselle Any, shall we say?'

'She's, well, she's very young, isn't she? Her father is a friend of Conrad's. She used to bring us apples, raspberries, cream . . .'

'And she wasn't in love with Cornelius?'

'No!'

That sounded definite.

'You didn't like her much?'

'Why wouldn't I? She came here, she laughed. She chattered all day long. Like a bird, you understand?'

'Do you know Oosting?'

'Yes.'

'Did he have any dealings with your husband?'

'Last year Oosting put a new engine into his boat. So he consulted Conrad. My husband drew up some plans for him. They went hunting for *zeehonden* – what do you call them in French? – seals, out on the sandbanks.'

And then suddenly:

'Oh, you think . . . The cap perhaps? It's impossible! Oosting!'

And she wailed, in distress once again:

'No, not Oosting. No! Nobody . . . Nobody could have killed Conrad. You didn't know him. He was . . . he . . .'

She turned her head aside, because she was weeping. Maigret preferred to leave. No one shook his hand and he simply bowed, muttering his apologies.

Outside, he was surprised by the damp coolness rising from the canal. And on the other bank, not far from the boatyard, he saw the Baes, talking to a student wearing the uniform of the Naval College.

They were both standing in the gathering dusk. Oosting seemed to be speaking insistently. The young man was looking down and only the pale oval of his face could be made out.

Maigret realized that this must be Cornelius. He was sure of it when he glimpsed a black armband on the blue woollen sleeve.

4. Logs on the Amsterdiep

He wasn't strictly speaking tailing them. At no time did Maigret have the feeling he was spying on anyone. He had been coming out of the Popinga house. He had walked a few steps. He had seen two men on the other side of the canal and had quite simply stopped to observe them. He wasn't hiding. He was there in full view on the bank, pipe in mouth and hands in pockets.

But perhaps it was precisely because he wasn't hiding, and because nevertheless the other men had not seen him as they carried on their intense conversation, that there was something poignant about that moment.

The bank on which the two men were standing was otherwise deserted. A shed loomed up in the centre of a dry dock where two boats were propped on stays, and a few dinghies lay rotting, hauled up out of the water.

On the canal itself, the floating tree trunks allowed only a metre or two of the liquid surface to be seen, giving the scene a slightly exotic feel.

It was evening now. In the semi-darkness, however, the air was still limpid, allowing the colours to retain all their clarity.

The tranquillity was surprisingly intense, so that the croaking of a frog in a distant marsh was startling.

The Baes was doing the talking. He did not raise his

voice. But he appeared to be enunciating each syllable clearly, wanting to be understood, or obeyed. Head lowered, the young man in his cadet uniform was listening. He was wearing white gloves, showing as the only bright spots in the failing light.

Suddenly there came an ear-splitting sound. A donkey had started to bray in a field somewhere behind Maigret. It was enough to break the charmed silence. Oosting, looking across in the direction of the animal, which was now beseeching the heavens, noticed Maigret, and let his gaze wander over him, but without showing any reaction.

He said a few more words to his companion, stuck the stem of his clay pipe in his mouth and set off towards the town.

It meant nothing, proved nothing. Maigret walked on as well, and the two men progressed in step together, one on either bank of the Amsterdiep.

But the path Oosting was taking soon diverged from the canalside. And the Baes presently disappeared behind some more sheds. For almost a minute, the heavy tread of his wooden clogs could still be heard.

It was night time now, scarcely a shred of light in the sky. The lamps had just been lit in town and along the canal, where the street lighting stopped at the Wienands' house. The other bank, uninhabited, remained in darkness.

Maigret turned round, without knowing why. He groaned as the donkey launched into another bout of desperate heehawing.

And he glimpsed further along, beyond the houses, two

little white patches dancing on the far side of the canal. Cornelius's gloves.

To a casual observer, especially one who forgot that the surface of the water was covered with logs, the sight would have been ghostly. Hands waving in the emptiness. The rest of the body melting into the night. And on the water the reflection of the furthest street lamp.

Oosting's footsteps could no longer be heard. Maigret walked back towards the outlying houses, passing once more in front of the Popingas' and then the Wienands' residence.

He was still making no effort to hide, but he realized that he too would have been swallowed up by the darkness. He followed the gloves with his eyes. Now he understood. To avoid going by way of Delfzijl, where there was a bridge over the canal, Cornelius was crossing the water using the floating logs as a raft. In the middle, there was a gap of about two metres. The white hands moved more quickly, went up in a rapid arc and the water splashed.

A few seconds later, he was walking along the bank, and being followed, scarcely a hundred metres behind, by Maigret.

It was not deliberate on either side, and in any case, Cornelius could not have been aware of the inspector's presence. All the same, from the first, they were walking in step, so that their crunching footfalls on the cinder path sounded in unison.

Maigret realized this, because his foot hit a stone at one point, and the synchronicity failed for a micro-second.

He didn't know where he was heading. And yet his pace

quickened as the young man speeded up. More than that: he felt he was gradually being dragged along in a sort of trance.

At first the steps ahead of him were long and regular. Then they shortened and became hurried.

Just as Cornelius was passing the timber yard, a veritable chorus of frogs broke out and the steps stopped abruptly.

Was Cornelius afraid of something? The footsteps continued, but even less regularly, sometimes hesitating, then on the contrary there would be two or three rapid paces, so that it seemed he might break into a run.

And now the silence was truly broken, as the frog chorus intensified. It filled the whole night air.

The steps accelerated. The same process started again. Maigret, by dint of walking in step with the other man, could literally sense his state of mind.

Cornelius was frightened! He was walking fast because he was afraid. He was anxious to get somewhere. But whenever he passed close to an unfamiliar-looking shadow, a stack of timber, a dead tree, a bush, his foot remained in the air a tenth of a second longer.

They reached a bend in the canal. A hundred metres ahead, going towards the farm, was the short stretch illuminated intermittently by the beam from the lighthouse. The young man seemed to be disconcerted by the bright swathe of light. He looked behind him. Then he rushed across it, again turning his head.

He had passed it, and was still casting backward glances, when Maigret calmly entered the illuminated zone, with all his bulk, presence and weight.

The cadet could not fail to see him. He stopped. Long enough to catch his breath. Then he set off again.

The light was behind them now. Ahead was a lit window, in the farm. Was the sound of the frogs following them? Although they were moving forward, it stayed close by, surrounding them, as if there were scores of the creatures escorting them.

A hundred metres from the house, a sudden final stop. A shadow detached itself from a tree trunk. A voice whispered.

Maigret had no wish to turn round and go back. That would be ridiculous. Nor did he want to hide. In any case it was too late, since he had walked through the lighthouse beam.

They knew he was there. He went forward slowly, unsettled now that there were no footsteps to echo his own.

The gloom was intense because of the thick foliage either side of the path. But a white glove showed up ahead, in movement.

An embrace. Cornelius's hand around the waist of a girl: Beetje.

Another fifty metres to go. Maigret paused for a moment, took some matches from his pocket and struck one to light his pipe, thus indicating his exact position.

Then he stepped forward. The lovers stirred. When he was no more than ten metres away, Beetje's silhouette detached itself and came to stand in the middle of the path, her face turned towards him, as if waiting for him. Cornelius stayed behind, flattening himself against a tree trunk.

Eight metres.

The window at the farm was still lit behind them. A plain reddish rectangle.

Suddenly there came a strangled cry, an indescribable cry of fear, indicating a loss of nerve, an utterance such as often precedes an outbreak of tearful sobs.

It was Cornelius weeping, his head in his hands, pressing himself against the tree as if for protection.

Beetje was standing in front of Maigret. She was wearing a coat, but the inspector noted that underneath she was in her nightdress, her legs were bare and her feet in bedroom slippers.

'Pay no attention!'

Well, this one was calm at any rate. Indeed she shot a glance at Cornelius, full of reproach and impatience.

The boy turned his back on them, trying to calm down. He couldn't manage it and was ashamed of his emotion.

'He's on edge . . . He thinks . . .'

'What does he think?'

'That he's going to be accused . . .'

Cornelius was still keeping his distance. He wiped his eyes. Was he about to make a break for it?

'I haven't accused anyone yet!' announced Maigret, for the sake of saying something.

'Of course not!'

And turning towards her companion, she spoke to him in Dutch. Maigret thought he understood, or guessed, that she was saying:

'You see? The inspector isn't accusing you. Calm down. This is childish!'

Then she suddenly stopped speaking. She stayed still,

listening. Maigret hadn't heard anything. A few seconds later, he thought he too could hear the snapping of a twig coming from the farm's direction. It was enough to rouse Cornelius, who looked round, his features drawn and his senses alerted.

Nobody spoke.

'Did you hear?' Beetje whispered. Cornelius tried to move towards the sound, with the bravado of a young cock. He was breathing heavily.

Too late. The enemy was nearer than they had realized.

Ten metres away, a figure loomed up, immediately recognizable: Farmer Liewens, in his carpet slippers.

'Beetje!' he called.

She did not dare answer at once. But as he repeated her name, she sighed, tremulously:

'Ja.'

Liewens was still coming forward. He walked past Cornelius, affecting not to notice him. Perhaps he had not yet seen Maigret?

But it was in front of the latter that he stopped four-square, eyes blazing and nostrils quivering with anger. He managed to contain himself, however. And stood quite still. When he spoke, his words were addressed to his daughter, in a harsh, peremptory voice.

Two or three sentences. She hung her head. Then he repeated the same word several times, in a commanding tone. Beetje spoke in French:

'He wants me to say to you . . .'

Her father was watching her as if to guess whether she was translating his words exactly.

'. . . that in Holland the police do not make arrangements to meet unmarried girls after dark out in the countryside.'

Maigret blushed as he had rarely had occasion to before. The rush of warm blood made his ears buzz.

What an idiotic accusation! And made in such bad faith!

Because there was Cornelius, skulking in the shadows, his eyes anxious and his shoulders hunched!

And Beetje's father must surely have known that it was to meet him that she had gone out. So? . . . What could he say in reply? Especially since he would have to go through an interpreter!

In any event, nobody waited for his answer. The father snapped his fingers as if to call a dog, and pointed out the path to his daughter, who hesitated, turned towards Maigret, did not dare look at her young admirer, and finally trudged away ahead of her father.

Cornelius hadn't moved. He raised a hand as if to stop the farmer's progress, but let it fall. Father and daughter disappeared into the distance. Shortly afterwards the farmhouse door slammed shut.

Had the frogs stopped croaking during this scene? It was hard to be sure, but their chorus now reached a deafening pitch.

'Do you speak French?'

'. . . Little bit.'

The cadet was looking at Maigret with dislike, opening his mouth to speak only reluctantly, and was standing sideways as if to offer less purchase to an attacker.

'Why are you so frightened?'

Tears sprang to his eyes, but there were no sobs.

Cornelius blew his nose at length. His hands were shaking. Was he going to have another panic attack?

'Do you really think you're going to be accused of killing your tutor?'

And Maigret added in a gruff voice:

'Come on, let's go.'

He pushed Cornelius in the direction of the town. He spoke slowly, sensing that his listener could only grasp about half his words.

'Is it for yourself that you're afraid?'

He was just a kid! A thin face with still unformed features, pale skin. Slender shoulders under the tight-fitting uniform. The cadet's cap was the finishing touch, making him look like a little boy dressed up as a sailor.

And distrust in his whole attitude, in the expression on his face. If Maigret had shouted at him, he would probably have raised his arms to fend off blows.

The black armband contributed a sombre and pitiful note to his appearance. It was only a month ago, wasn't it, that this boy had learned that his mother had died in the East Indies, perhaps one night when he had been enjoying himself in Delfzijl, possibly even at the annual college ball?

He would be going home in two years, with the rank of third officer, and his father would show him a grave already overgrown, and maybe another woman installed in the family home.

And his life would begin on some great steamship: watches on deck, ports of call, Java–Rotterdam, Rotterdam–Java, two days here, five or six hours there.

'Where were you when your teacher was shot?'

Now a terrible heart-wrenching sob. The boy seized Maigret's lapels in his white-gloved hands, which were trembling convulsively.

'No, not true! Not true,' he repeated a dozen or more times. '*Nee!* You not understand. No, no. Not true!'

They had reached the patch of light beamed out by the lighthouse once more. The brightness dazzled them, outlining their shapes, making every detail stand out.

'Where were you?'

'Over there.'

Over there was the Popinga house, and the canal, which he must have been in the habit of crossing by jumping from log to log.

This was an important detail. Popinga had died at five to midnight. Cornelius had reported back to his ship at five past midnight. The usual route, through the town, would take at least thirty minutes.

But it would take only six or seven minutes crossing the canal this way, avoiding the long detour!

Maigret kept walking with his deliberate, heavy tread, beside the young man, who was trembling like a leaf, and when the donkey started braying again, Cornelius jumped, quivering from head to toe as if he were about to run away.

'You're in love with Beetje?'

A stubborn silence.

'And you saw her come back, after your tutor had seen her home?'

'That's not true. Not true.'

Maigret was on the point of calming him down with a good shaking.

And yet he looked at him with an indulgent, perhaps affectionate air.

'You see Beetje every day?'

Another silence.

'What time are you supposed to be back on the college boat?'

'Ten . . . If not permission. When I went my tutor, me can . . .'

'Be back later? But not tonight?'

They were standing on the bank, near the place where Cornelius had crossed the canal. Maigret headed for the tree trunks, in the most natural way in the world, put his foot on the first and almost fell into the water, because he wasn't used to it and the log rolled under his foot.

'Come on. It'll soon be ten o'clock.'

The boy looked astonished. He must have been expecting never to see his college boat again, and to be arrested and thrown into jail.

And now this terrible French inspector was escorting him back, and preparing, like him, to jump over the two-metre gap in the middle of the canal. They splashed each other. On the other bank, Maigret stopped to wipe his trouser leg.

'Where is it?'

He hadn't explored this bank yet. There was a large area of wasteland between the Amsterdiep and the new canal, which was wide, deep and navigable by sea-going vessels.

Looking behind him, the inspector could see a single

window lit on the first floor of the Popinga house. A figure, Any's, was moving behind the curtains. It must be Popinga's study. But he couldn't guess what the young lawyer was doing.

Cornelius had calmed down a little.

'I swear . . .' he began.

'No!'

That took him aback.

He stared at the inspector with such a wild-eyed expression that Maigret tapped him on the shoulder, saying:

'Never swear to anything. Especially in your situation. Would you have wanted to marry Beetje?'

'Ja, oh ja!'

'And would her father have agreed to that?'

Silence. Head down, Cornelius kept on walking, threading his way among the old boats hauled up on the shore.

The broad surface of the Ems canal came into sight. At the bend a large black-and-white vessel loomed up, with every porthole illuminated. A high prow. Mast and rigging.

It was a former Dutch navy vessel, a hundred years old, now no longer seaworthy but moored here as accommodation for the students at the Naval College.

Around it moved some dark silhouettes and the glow of cigarette ends. The sound of a piano came from the games room.

Suddenly the peal of a hand bell was heard, and all the silhouettes on the bank merged into a crowd around the gangway, while further down the path from the town, four stragglers were returning at a run.

It was like the sight at a school gate, except that all these young men aged between sixteen and twenty-two were in the uniform of naval officers, with white gloves and stiff peaked caps trimmed with gold braid.

A grizzled quartermaster, leaning on the guardrail, watched them filing in while he smoked his pipe.

A youthful scene, lively and full of fun. Jokes that Maigret couldn't understand were exchanged. Cigarettes were flung down as the gangway was reached. And on board there were mock fights, chases.

The last arrivals, out of breath, were reaching the foot of the gangway. Cornelius, red-eyed, his features drawn and his expression anguished, turned to Maigret.

'Go on, get along with you,' grunted the inspector.

The boy understood his gesture better than his words, put his hand to his peaked cap, made a clumsy military salute and opened his mouth to say something.

'That'll do! Get going.'

Because the quartermaster was on the point of going inside, while a student was taking up his post as sentry. Through the portholes, the young men could be seen shaking out hammocks, throwing their clothes around with abandon.

Maigret stayed where he was until he had seen Cornelius go timidly into the dormitory, looking awkward, with hunched shoulders – and receive a pillow full in the face before he went over to a hammock at the back of the cabin.

Another scene was about to begin, a more picturesque one. The inspector had gone no more than a dozen paces towards the town when he saw Oosting who, like himself, had come to watch the cadets going back.

The two men were both middle-aged, heavily built and calm.

They surely looked ridiculous, both of them, observing the youngsters climbing into their hammocks and having pillow-fights.

They were for all the world like mother-hens, weren't they, keeping watch over a wayward chick?

They glanced at each other. The Baes did not move, but touched the peak of his cap.

They knew that any conversation was impossible, since neither spoke the other's language.

But, '*Goedenavond*,' muttered the man from Workum.

'*Bonne nuit*,' said Maigret, as if echoing him.

They were going in the same direction, following a path which after about two hundred metres turned into a road, leading into town.

They were now walking along side by side. To separate, one of them would have had to slow his pace deliberately, and neither wanted to do so.

Oosting in his clogs, Maigret in his city clothes. Both men were smoking pipes, only Maigret's was a briar, the Baes's made of china clay.

The third building they came to was a café, and Oosting went in, after stamping his clogs and then leaving them on the doormat, as was the Dutch custom.

Maigret thought for no more than a second before entering in turn.

A dozen or so seamen and bargees sat around the same table, smoking pipes and cigars, and drinking beer or genever.

Oosting shook a few hands, pulled up a chair on which he sat down heavily, and listened to the general conversation.

Maigret settled himself off to one side, well aware that in fact attention was focused on him. The proprietor, who was sitting with the group, waited a few moments before coming to ask him what he would have to drink.

The genever came from a porcelain and brass fountain. This was the predominant smell, peculiar to all Dutch cafés, making the atmosphere very different from a café in France.

Oosting's small eyes were full of laughter every time he looked at the inspector.

Maigret stretched his legs, brought them back under his chair, stretched them again, and stuffed his pipe, all to give himself an impression of composure. The café owner got up to come and offer him a light in person.

'*Mooi weer!*'

Maigret, having no idea what this meant, frowned, and had it repeated.

'*Mooi weer, ja . . . Oost wind.*'

Everyone else waited, nudging each other. Someone pointed at the window, at the starry sky.

'*Mooi weer* . . . Fair weather.'

And he tried to explain that the wind was in the east, which was a very good sign.

Oosting was selecting a cigar from a box. He fingered five or six placed in front of him. He conspicuously chose a Manila one, as black as coal, and spat the end on the floor before lighting up.

Then he showed his new cap to his companions.

'Vier gulden.'

Four florins! Forty francs! His eyes were still laughing.

But someone came in, opening a newspaper and talking about the latest freight prices on the Amsterdam Stock Exchange.

And in the animated conversation that followed, which sounded like a quarrel because of the deep voices and harsh syllables, they forgot about Maigret, who took some change from his pocket, then went off to bed in the Van Hasselt Hotel.

5. Jean Duclos's Theories

From the hotel café, as he ate his breakfast next morning, Maigret witnessed the search, about which he had not been informed in advance. Admittedly, he hadn't attempted more than a brief meeting with the Dutch police.

It was about eight o'clock. The mist had not quite cleared, but one sensed that the sun was about to break through, ushering in a fine day. A Finnish cargo ship was leaving port, pulled by a tug. In front of the little café on the corner of the quayside, a large conclave of men had gathered, in their clogs and seaman's caps, talking in small groups.

This was the daily commodities exchange of the *schippers*, the owners of the sea-going barges of every size, crowded with wives and children, which filled one basin in the harbour.

Further along stood another handful of men: the Quayside Rats. And two uniformed gendarmes had just arrived. They had stepped on to the deck of Oosting's boat, and he himself had emerged from the forward hatch, since when he was in Delfzijl he always slept on board.

A man in civilian clothes now arrived: Inspector Pijpekamp, officially in charge of the case. He took off his hat and spoke politely. The two gendarmes vanished inside.

The search was beginning. All the *schippers* had seen it.

But there wasn't the slightest movement from them, not even any show of curiosity.

Nor did the Quayside Rats budge an inch. Just a few glances, that was all.

It lasted a good half-hour. When they emerged, the gendarmes gave a military salute. Pijpekamp seemed to be apologizing.

Only, this particular morning, the Baes did not seem to want to come ashore. Instead of joining his friends on the quay, he sat down on a thwart, crossed one leg over the other, looked out to sea, where the Finnish vessel was moving heavily along, and remained there motionless, smoking his pipe.

When Maigret turned round, Jean Duclos was coming downstairs from his room, carrying a briefcase and an armful of books and folders, which he placed on the table he had reserved.

He merely looked questioningly at Maigret, without any greeting.

'Well?'

'Well, I think I should wish you good morning.'

The other man stared at him in some surprise and shrugged his shoulders, as if to say: not worth getting bothered about.

'Have you discovered anything?'

'Have you?'

'You know that, in theory, I'm not supposed to leave here. Your Dutch colleague has fortunately understood that my knowledge might be helpful to him, so I have been kept informed of the results of the investigation. That's a practice the French police might like to take as an example . . .'

'Oh for goodness' sake!'

The professor hurried towards Madame Van Hasselt as she entered the room with her hair in rollers, greeted her as he would have done in a polite drawing room and apparently enquired after her health.

Maigret looked at the papers spread out on the table and recognized a new set of plans and diagrams, not only of the Popinga house but of almost the whole town, with dotted lines drawn on them which must indicate the paths taken by certain persons.

The sun, shining through the multicoloured stained-glass windows, filled the glossy-panelled room with green, red and blue shafts of light. A brewer's dray had pulled up at the door, and during the entire conversation that followed, two gigantic men were rolling barrels continuously across the floor under the eye of Madame Van Hasselt in her early-morning attire. Never had the mingled aromas of genever and beer been so overpowering. And never had Maigret been so aware of the smell of Holland.

'You've identified the murderer, then?' he asked with a sly smile, pointing to the papers.

A sharp glance from Duclos. And his reply:

'I'm beginning to think the foreigners are right. A Frenchman is above all someone who cannot resist irony. Well, in this case, monsieur, it is out of place.'

Maigret looked at him, still smiling, and in no way put out of countenance. The other man went on:

'No, I haven't found the murderer. But I have perhaps

done more. I've analysed the situation, I've dissected it. I have isolated each element of it . . . and now . . .'

'Now . . . ?'

'Now, someone like you will no doubt profit from my deductions and wrap up the case.'

He had seated himself. He was determined to talk, in spite of the atmosphere which he himself had made unfriendly. Maigret sat down opposite him and ordered a Bols.

'I'm listening.'

'You will notice in the first place that I am not even asking you what you have done, or what you think. I'll start with the first potential suspect: myself. I had, if I may say so, the best strategic position to shoot Popinga, and besides I was seen holding the murder weapon a few moments after the attack.

'I'm not a rich man, and if my name is known throughout the whole world, or almost, it is only by a small number of intellectuals. I am a man of modest means and sometimes living in straitened circumstances. But there was no theft, and in no way could I have hoped to benefit from the death of a lecturer at the Naval College.

'But wait! That doesn't mean that charges against me can be dropped. And people will not fail to recall that in the course of the evening, since we were discussing forensic science, I defended the proposition that an intelligent man who wished to commit a crime in cold blood might, using all his faculties, outwit a poorly educated police force.

'From which they might deduce that I had sought to illustrate my theory by example. Between ourselves, I can categorically state that if that were the case, the possibility of suspecting me would never have arisen.'

'Your good health,' said Maigret, who was watching the bull-necked brewers' men come and go.

'To continue. I postulate that if I did not commit the crime, and yet the crime was nevertheless committed, as everything seems to indicate, by someone in the house, then the whole family is guilty.

'Don't look startled! Examine my plan of the house. And above all, try to understand the psychological considerations, which I am about to develop.

This time, Maigret could not suppress a smile at the professor's scornful condescension.

'You have no doubt heard that Madame Popinga, née Van Elst, belongs to the strictest sect in the Reformed Church. In Amsterdam, her father is known as the fiercest of conservatives. And her sister Any, already, at twenty-five, has similar ideas in politics.

'You only arrived here yesterday, and there are many aspects of Dutch life with which you are not yet familiar. Did you know that a teacher at the Naval College would receive a severe reprimand from his superiors if he were seen entering a café like this one? One of them lost his job, merely because he persisted in subscribing to a newspaper suspected of advanced views.

'I met Popinga only that one evening. But it was enough, especially after having heard what people said about him. A likely lad, you might call him. A rollicking likely lad! With his round cheeks and his bright eyes full of fun . . .

'You need to understand he had been a sailor. And when

he came back ashore, he had, in a sense, put on the uniform of austerity. But the uniform was bursting at the seams.

'Do you see what I mean? It will make you smile. Because you're French. A couple of weeks ago, the club he belongs to held one of its regular meetings. Since Dutchmen don't go out to cafés at night, they get together in a hired room, under the pretext of club membership, to play billiards or skittles.

'Well, two weeks ago, by eleven at night, Popinga was quite drunk. In the same week, his wife had been organizing collections to buy clothes for the native peoples in the East Indies. And there was Popinga, with his red cheeks and shiny eyes, saying: "Waste of time! They look much better with no clothes on! Instead of buying clothes for them, we should do as they do . . ."

'Well, of course you're smiling. A silly remark that means nothing at all. But the scandal is still raging, and if Popinga's funeral is held in Delfzijl, some people will avoid going to it.

'And that's just one little incident. Plenty more where that came from! As I said, every one of the seams of Popinga's uniform of respectability was bursting open. Just try to work out what a sin it is here to get drunk! And his pupils had seen him in that state. That was probably why they were so fond of him!

'And now, try to imagine the atmosphere in that house on the banks of the Amsterdiep. Think of Madame Popinga and Any.

'Look out of the window. On both sides you can see to the edge of the town. It's tiny. Everyone knows everyone else. Scandal takes about an hour to reach the entire population. Including Popinga's relations with the man they call the Baes, and who is a kind of brigand, I have to say. They went seal-hunting together. And Popinga used to knock back spirits on Oosting's boat.

'I'm not asking you to come to a conclusion right away. I would just repeat this sentence: *if the crime was committed by someone in the house, the whole house is guilty.*

'Then there is that silly little girl, Beetje. Popinga never missed a chance of seeing her home. Shall I give you an idea of what she's like? Beetje is the only female round here who goes swimming every day, and not wearing a decent bathing-dress with a skirt, like all the other ladies, but in a skin-tight costume. Bright red, what's more!

'I'll let you carry on with your inquiries. I just wanted to give you a few elements that the police tend to overlook.

'As for Cornelius Barens, as I see it, he's part of the family, on the female side.

'So on one hand, if you like, you have Madame Popinga, her sister Any and Cornelius. On the other, Beetje, Oosting and Popinga. If you have understood what I've told you, you might get somewhere.'

'Can I ask you a question?' said Maigret gravely.

'Yes, I'm listening.'

'Are you a Protestant too?'

'I am, yes, but I don't belong to the *Dutch* Reformed Church. It isn't the same . . .'

'So which side of the barricades are you on?'

'I didn't like Popinga . . .'

'So . . .'

'I disapprove of crime, of whatever kind.'

'Didn't he play jazz music and dance while you were talking to the ladies?'

'That's another aspect of his character that I didn't think to tell you about.'

Maigret looked splendidly serious, solemn indeed, as he stood up, saying:

'So in sum, who do you advise me to arrest?'

Professor Duclos gave a start.

'I didn't mention arresting anyone. I have given you some general indications in the realm of pure ideas, if I may say so.'

'Of course. But in my place . . . ?'

'I'm not the police. I am looking for truth for truth's sake and even the fact that I am myself under suspicion is not capable of influencing my judgement.'

'So I shouldn't arrest anyone?'

'I didn't say that, I . . .'

'Thank you,' said Maigret, extending his hand.

And he tapped his glass with a coin to call Madame Van Hasselt over. Duclos looked at him disapprovingly.

'Not the kind of thing one should do here,' he murmured. 'At least not if you want to be taken for a gentleman.'

The trapdoor for rolling the beer barrels into the cellar was being closed. Maigret paid his bill, and gave a last glance at the plans.

'So, either you, or the whole family . . .'

'I didn't say that. Listen . . .'

But Maigret was already at the door. Once his back was turned, he allowed his features to relax, and if he didn't burst out laughing at least he had a delighted smile on his face.

Outside he found himself bathed in sunlight, gentle warmth and calm. The ironmonger was at the door of his workshop. The little Jewish chandler was counting his anchors and marking them with red paint.

The crane was still unloading coal. Several *schippers* were hoisting their sails, not because they were leaving, but to allow the canvas to dry. And among the forest of masts they looked like great curtains, brown and white, flapping gently in the breeze.

Oosting was smoking his clay pipe on the afterdeck of his boat. A few Quayside Rats were chatting quietly.

But turning towards the town, one could see the smug residences of the local bourgeoisie, freshly painted, with their sparkling panes, immaculate net curtains and pot plants in every window. Beyond those windows, impenetrable shadows.

Perhaps the scene had taken on a new meaning since his conversation with Jean Duclos.

On one hand, the port, the men in clogs, the boats and sails, the tang of tar and salt water.

On the other, those houses with their polished furniture and dark wall-hangings, where people could gossip behind closed doors for a fortnight about a lecturer at the Naval College who had had a glass too many one evening.

The same sky, of heavenly limpidity. But what a frontier between these two worlds!

Then Maigret imagined Popinga, whom he had never seen, even in death, but who had had a ruddy round face, reflecting his crude appetites.

He imagined him standing at that frontier, gazing at

Oosting's boat, or at some five-master whose crew had put in to every port in South America, or perhaps at the Dutch steamers that had plied in China alongside junks full of slim women who looked like beautiful porcelain dolls.

And all he had was an English dinghy, highly varnished and fitted with brass trimmings, to sail the flat waters of the Amsterdiep, where you had to navigate through floating tree trunks from Scandinavia or some tropical rainforest!

It seemed to Maigret that the Baes was looking at him meaningfully, as if he would have liked to come over and talk to him. But that was impossible! They would have been unable to exchange two words.

Oosting knew that, and stayed where he was, simply puffing a little faster on his pipe, his eyelids half-closed in the sunlight.

At this time of day, Cornelius Barens would be sitting on a college bench, listening to a lecture on trigonometry or astronomy. No doubt he was still pale in the face.

Maigret was about to go and sit on a bronze bollard when he saw Pijpekamp coming towards him, hand held out.

'Did you find anything this morning aboard the boat?'

'Not yet . . . It's just a formality.'

'You suspect Oosting?'

'Well, there was the cap . . .'

'And the cigar!'

'No. The Baes only smokes Brazilian cigars, and that was a Manila.'

'So?'

Pijpekamp drew him further along the quay, so as not to be under the nose of the overlord of Workum Island.

'The compass on board used to belong to a ship from Helsingfors. The lifebelts came from an English collier . . . And there's plenty more like that . . .'

'Stolen?'

'No. It's always the way. Whenever a cargo vessel comes into the port, there's invariably someone, an engineer, a third officer, an ordinary seaman, sometimes even the captain, who wants to sell something. You see? They tell the company that the lifebelts were swept overboard in a storm, or that the compass didn't work. Emergency flares, whatever you can think of. Sometimes even a dinghy!'

'So that doesn't prove anything.'

'No. See the Jewish chandler over there, he makes his living from this second-hand trade.'

'So your investigation . . .'

Pijpekamp turned away, looking awkward.

'I told you that Beetje Liewens hadn't gone straight home. She retraced her footsteps. That's how you say it, yes? In French?'

'Yes, yes, go on!'

'Maybe she didn't fire the gun . . .'

'Ah.'

The Dutchman was definitely ill at ease. He felt the need to drop his voice, and to take Maigret towards a completely deserted part of the quayside before going on.

'There's that timber yard . . . You see what I mean. The *timmerman* . . . In French you say the sawyer, so, yes, the sawyer claims he saw Beetje and Monsieur Popinga. Yes. The two of them.'

'Hiding behind a stack of timber, you mean?'

'Yes, and I think . . .'

'You think . . . ?'

'There may have been two other people nearby. That's the thing. The boy from the college, Cornelius Barens. He's been wanting to marry that girl. We found a photo of her in his satchel.'

'Really?'

'And also Monsieur Liewens, Beetje's father. Very important man. He raises cattle for export. He even sends some to Australia. He's a widower, and she's his only child.'

'So *he* might have killed Popinga?'

Pijpekamp was so embarrassed that Maigret almost felt sorry for him. It was clearly very painful for him to accuse an important man, someone who raised cattle for export to Australia, no less.

'If he saw, you know . . .'

Maigret was relentless.

'If he saw what?'

'Near the timber stacks. Beetje and Popinga . . .'

'Ah yes.'

'This is completely confidential . . .'

'Good Lord, yes. But what about Barens?'

'He might have seen them too. And perhaps he was jealous. But he was back in college five minutes after the shooting. That's what I don't understand.'

'So to sum up,' said Maigret, in the same solemn tones

he had used when speaking to Duclos, 'you suspect both Beetje's father and her admirer, Cornelius.'

There was an awkward silence.

'And you also suspect Oosting, whose cap was found in the bath.'

Pijpekamp made a gesture of discouragement.

'And of course, there's also the man who left a Manila cheroot in the dining room. How many cigar shops are there in Delfzijl?'

'Fifteen.'

'That doesn't help. And finally, you suspect Professor Duclos.'

'Because he was holding the gun. I can't allow him to leave. You do see that.'

'Absolutely!'

They walked on about fifty metres in silence.

'So what do you think?' said the Groningen policeman, at last.

'That is the question. And that's the difference between us. You think something. In fact, you think a great many things. But I'm not aware of thinking anything yet.'

Then suddenly a question:

'Did Beetje Liewens know the Baes?'

'I don't know. I don't think so.'

'Did Cornelius know him?'

Pijpekamp rubbed his forehead.

'Maybe, maybe not. Probably not. I can find out.'

'That's it. Try to find out if they were acquainted at all before the murder.'

'You think . . . ?'

'I don't think anything at all. One more question. Can they get wireless reception on Workum?'

'No idea.'

'Another thing to find out, then.'

It was hard to say quite how it had happened, but now there was a kind of hierarchy between Maigret and his companion, who was looking up to him almost as if he were his superior officer.

'So, concentrate on those two things. I'm going to pay a visit . . .'

Pijpekamp was too polite to ask any questions about the visit, but his eyes were full of curiosity.

'. . . to Mademoiselle Beetje,' Maigret went on. 'What's the quickest way?'

'Along the Amsterdiep.'

They could see the Delfzijl pilot boat, a handsome steam vessel of some 500 tons, describing a curve on the Ems before entering port. And the Baes, walking with a slow but heavy tread, full of pent-up emotion, on the deck of his boat, a hundred metres from where the Quayside Rats were soaking up the sunshine.

6. The Letters

It was purely by chance that Maigret did not follow the Amsterdiep, but took the cross-country path.

The farm, in the morning sunshine of eleven o'clock, reminded him of his first steps on Dutch soil, the girl in her shiny boots in the modern cowshed, the prim and proper parlour and the teapot in its quilted cosy.

The same calm reigned now. Very far away, almost at the limit of the infinite horizon, a large brown sail floated above the field looking like some ghost ship sailing in an ocean of grassland.

As it had the first time, the dog barked. A good five minutes passed before the door opened, and then only a few centimetres wide, enough to let him guess at the red-cheeked face and gingham apron of the maidservant.

And even so, she was on the point of shutting the door before Maigret could even speak.

'Mademoiselle Liewens!' he called.

The garden separated them. The old woman stayed in the doorway and the inspector was on the other side of the gate. Between them, the dog was watching the intruder and baring its teeth.

The servant shook her head. 'She isn't here . . . *Niet hier.*'

Maigret had by now picked up a few words in Dutch. 'And monsieur . . . *Mijnheer?*'

A final negative sign and the door closed. But as the inspector did not go away immediately, it budged, just a few millimetres this time, and Maigret guessed the old woman was spying on him.

If he was lingering, it was because he had seen a curtain stir at the window he knew to be that of the daughter of the house. Behind the curtain, the blur of a face. Hard to see, but what Maigret did make out was a slight hand movement, which might have been a simple greeting, but more probably meant: 'I'm here. Don't insist. Watch out.'

The old woman behind the door meant one thing. This pale hand another. As did the dog jumping up at the gate and barking. All around, the cows in the fields looked artificial in their stillness.

Maigret risked a little experiment. He took a couple of steps forward, as if to go through the gate after all. He could not resist a smile, since not only did the door shut hurriedly, but even the dog, so fierce before, withdrew, tail between its legs.

This time the inspector did leave, taking the Amsterdiep towpath. All that this reception had told him was that Beetje had been confined to the house, and that orders had been given by the farmer not to let the Frenchman in.

Maigret puffed thoughtfully at his pipe. He looked for a moment at the stacks of timber where Beetje and Popinga had stopped, probably many times, holding their bicycles with one hand, while embracing each other with a free arm.

And what still dominated the scene was the calm. A serene, almost too perfect calm. A calm that might make a Frenchman believe that all of life here was as artificial as a picture postcard.

For instance, he turned round suddenly and saw only a few metres away a high-stemmed boat, which he had not heard approaching. He recognized the sail, which was wider than the canal. It was the same sail he had seen only a short time ago far away on the horizon, and yet it was here already, without it seeming possible that it could have covered the distance so quickly.

At the helm was a woman, a baby at her breast, nudging the tiller with her hip. And a man sat astride the bowsprit, legs hanging over the water, while he repaired the bobstay.

The boat glided past first the Wienands' house, then that of the Popingas, and the sail was higher than either roof. For a moment, it hid the entire façade, with its huge moving shadow.

Once again, Maigret stopped. He hesitated. The Popingas' maidservant was on her knees, scrubbing the front step, head down, hips in the air, and the door stood open.

She gave a start as she sensed him behind her. The hand holding the floor cloth was shaking.

'Madame Popinga?' he said, indicating the interior of the house.

She tried to go ahead of him, but she got up awkwardly, because of the cloth, which was dripping with dirty water. He was the first to enter the corridor. Hearing a man's voice in the parlour, he knocked at the door.

There was a sudden silence. A total, uncompromising silence. And more than silence: expectation, as if life had been momentarily suspended.

Then footsteps. A hand touched the doorknob from inside. The door began to move. Maigret saw first of all Any, who had just opened it for him, and who gave him an unfriendly stare. Then he made out the silhouette of a man standing at the table, wearing a thick tweed suit and tawny gaiters.

Farmer Liewens.

And finally, leaning her elbow on the mantelpiece and shielding her face with her hand, Madame Popinga.

It was clear that the intruder's arrival had interrupted an important conversation, a dramatic scene, probably an argument.

On the table covered with a lace cloth, some letters were randomly scattered, as if they had been thrown down violently.

The farmer's face was the most animated, but it was also the countenance that froze most immediately.

'I'm afraid I'm disturbing you . . .' Maigret began.

Nobody spoke. Not a word from anyone. Only Madame Popinga, after a tearful glance round, left the room and went almost at a run towards the kitchen.

'Please believe that I am very sorry to have interrupted your conversation.'

At last Liewens spoke, in Dutch. He addressed a few evidently cutting remarks to the young woman, and Maigret could not help asking:

'What does he say?'

'That he will be back. That the French police . . .'

She looked embarrassed as she cast about for a way to continue.

'. . . have incredibly bad manners, perhaps,' Maigret finished the sentence. 'We have already had occasion to meet, Monsieur Liewens and I.'

The other man tried to guess what they were saying, paying attention to Maigret's intonation and expression. And the inspector, for his part, let his eyes fall on to the letters and on the signature at the bottom of one of them: *Conrad*.

The embarrassment was now at its height. The farmer moved to pick up his cap from a chair, but could not resign himself to leaving.

'He has just brought you letters that your brother-in-law wrote to his daughter.'

'How did you know?'

For heaven's sake! The scene was so easy to reconstruct, in that atmosphere thick with emotion: Liewens arriving, holding his breath in his efforts to contain his anger. Liewens being shown into the parlour, and into the presence of the two terrified women, then suddenly speaking to them and throwing the letters on the table. Madame Popinga, distraught, hiding her face in her hands, perhaps refusing to believe the evidence, or so distressed that she was unable to speak. And Any trying to stand up to the man, arguing . . .

And it was at this point that he had knocked on the door. Everyone had frozen and Any had let him in.

In his reconstruction of events, Maigret was mistaken in one respect at least, the character of one of the people concerned. For Madame Popinga, whom he imagined to be in the kitchen, devastated by this revelation, completely overcome and without any strength, entered the room a few moments later with a calm bearing such as is reached only at a high pitch of emotion.

And slowly, she too put some letters on the table. She did not throw them down. She placed them deliberately. She looked at the farmer and then at the inspector.

She opened her mouth several times before managing to speak and then said:

'You will have to judge for yourselves . . . Someone should read these out . . .'

At that moment, Liewens blushed a deep scarlet as blood rushed to his cheeks. He was too Dutch to fall on the letters at once, but they drew him as if by an irresistible spell.

A woman's handwriting. Blue paper . . . Letters from Beetje, obviously. One thing was immediately striking: the disproportion between the two piles of letters. There were perhaps ten notes from Popinga, always written on a single sheet of paper, and usually consisting of four or five lines.

There were about thirty letters from Beetje, long and closely written!

Conrad was dead. And there remained these two unequal piles of letters, as well as the stack of timber that had protected the couple's rendezvous, on the banks of the Amsterdiep.

'Best if everyone calms down,' said Maigret. 'And perhaps it would be preferable to read out these letters without getting too angry.'

The farmer stared at him, with remarkable sharpness,

and must have understood since he took a step towards the table, in spite of himself.

Maigret leaned on to the table with both hands, and picked up a note from Popinga at random.

'Would you have the goodness to translate this, please, Mademoiselle Any?'

But the young woman did not seem to hear him. She looked down at the writing, without speaking. Her sister, serious and dignified, took the letter from her hands.

'It was written at college,' she said. 'There's no date, just six o'clock. This is what it says:

Dear little Beetje,
    Better if you don't come tonight as the college principal is coming round for a cup of tea. See you tomorrow.
    Love and kisses.

She looked around with an air of calm defiance. Then she picked up another note. She read it out slowly:

Dear pretty little Beetje,
    You must calm down. And remember that life is long. I've got a lot of work to do with the third-year exams. I can't come tonight.
    Why do you keep saying I don't love you? I can't leave the college. What on earth would we do?
    Take it easy, I beg you. We've got plenty of time.
    With affectionate kisses.

And as Maigret seemed to say that that was enough, Madame Popinga took up another letter:

'There's this one, probably the last.'

My dear Beetje,

It's impossible. I beg you to be sensible. You know perfectly well that I don't have any money and that it would take a long time to find employment abroad.

You must be more careful and not get so wrought up. And above all, trust me.

Don't be afraid. If what you are worried about happens, I'll do my duty.

I'm anxious because I've got a lot of work on just now, and when I think of you, I can't work properly. The principal passed a critical remark yesterday and I was very upset.

I'll try to get out tomorrow evening, and tell them I'm going to visit a Norwegian ship in port.

I embrace you fondly, little Beetje.

Madame Popinga looked at each of them in turn, wearily, her eyes hooded. Her hand moved to the other pile, the one she had brought in, and the farmer gave a start. She pulled out a letter.

Dear Conrad, that I love so much,

Good news: Papa has put another thousand florins in my bank account for my birthday present. That's enough to get to America, because I looked up the boat fares in the newspaper. And we could travel third class!

But why don't you hurry up? I can't live here any more. Holland is stifling me to death. The people in Delfzijl seem to be staring at me with disapproval all the time.

But I'm so proud and happy to belong to a man like you! We must absolutely get away before the holidays because Papa wants me to spend a month in Switzerland and I don't want to. Otherwise our big project would have to wait till winter.

I've been buying English books. I can say lots of sentences already. Hurry up, do! We'll have such a lovely time, the two of us. Won't we? We can't stay here. Especially now. I think Madame Popinga is giving me the cold shoulder. And I'm still afraid of Cornelius, who is courting me, and I don't seem able to discourage him. He's a nice boy and polite, but really stupid.

And of course he's not a man, Conrad, not a real man like you: you've been everywhere, you know everything.

Remember, a year ago, I used to try and meet you on the road and you didn't even look at me!

And now, maybe I'm going to have your child! Or anyway, it's possible.

But why are you being so cool? Don't you love me as much as before?

That wasn't the end of the letter, but Madame Popinga's voice had died away in her throat and she stopped speaking. She leafed through the pile of correspondence with her fingers. She was looking for something.

She read out one more sentence from the middle of a letter:

... and I'm starting to think you love your wife more than me, I'm beginning to feel jealous of her and to hate her. If that isn't the reason, why would you be saying now you don't want to go away?

The farmer could not understand the French words, but he was paying such close attention that anyone would have sworn he could guess. Madame Popinga swallowed hard, picked up one last sheet, and read in an even more strained voice:

I've heard rumours that Cornelius is more in love with Madame Popinga than with me, and that they are getting on very well. If only that were true! Then we'd be left in peace and you wouldn't have to feel bad about it.

The sheet dropped from her hands and floated down on to the carpet in front of Any, who stared at it fixedly.

There was another silence. Madame Popinga was not weeping. But everything about her was tragic: her contained pain, her dignity, maintained only through incredible effort, the admirable sentiment which had inspired her.

She had come to defend Conrad! She was waiting for an attack. She would fight if she had to.

'When did you discover these letters?' Maigret asked, awkwardly.

'The day after . . .'

She choked. She opened her mouth for a gulp of air. Her eyelids were swollen.

'. . . after Conrad . . .'

'I see.'

He understood. He looked at her with sympathy. She was not pretty. And yet she had regular features. Her face had none of the flaws that made Any's so unprepossessing.

Madame Popinga was a tall woman, well-built, but not fat. A glossy helmet of fine hair framed her delicately pink Dutch face.

But would he perhaps have preferred it if she had been ugly? Those regular features and her controlled, sensible expression somehow conveyed a total lack of enthusiasm for life.

Even her smile had to be a sensible, measured smile, her joy a sensible joy, always under control.

Already at six years old, she must have been a serious child. And by sixteen, much as she was today.

One of those women who seem born to be sisters, or aunts, or nurses, or widows patronizing good causes.

Conrad was no longer there, and yet Maigret had never felt him to be so alive as at this moment, with his hearty open face, his greed or rather appetite for life, his shyness, his fear of offending people and his wireless set, with which he fiddled for hours in order to pick up jazz from Paris, gypsy music from Budapest, an operetta from Vienna, or perhaps even faraway boat-to-boat calls on short wave.

Any approached her sister, as one would someone who is ill and about to collapse. But Madame Popinga went towards Maigret, or at least took a couple of steps.

'I never dreamed . . .' she whispered. 'Never. I lived . . . I . . . And when he died, I . . .'

He guessed, from her breathing, that she had a heart

condition, and a moment later she confirmed his hypothesis by standing still for a long moment, pressing her hand to her chest.

Someone else moved in the room: the farmer, with wild eyes and a fevered expression, had gone over to the table and snatched up the letters from his daughter, with the nervous gesture of a thief fearing to be caught.

She let him go ahead. Maigret did the same.

But Liewens did not yet dare leave. He could be heard speaking, without addressing anyone in particular. Maigret caught the word *Fransman*, and it was as if he could understand Dutch in the same way that Liewens, that day, had understood French.

He could more or less work out the sentence: 'And you think it was necessary to tell the Frenchman all this?'

Liewens dropped his cap, picked it up, bowed to Any, who was standing in his way, but to her alone, muttered a few more unintelligible syllables and went out. The maid must have finished cleaning the step since they heard the door open and shut and his footsteps going away.

In spite of the younger woman's presence, Maigret asked some further questions, with a gentleness one might not have suspected in him.

'Have you already shown these letters to your sister?'

'No. But when that man . . .'

'Where were they?'

'In a drawer in the bedside table . . . I never used to open it. It was where the revolver was kept too.'

Any said something in Dutch, and Madame Popinga translated automatically.

'My sister is telling me I ought to go and lie down. Because I haven't slept for three nights. He'd never have gone away from here . . . He must have been imprudent, just one indiscretion, don't you think? He liked to laugh and play. But now that I think of it, some little things come back . . . Beetje used to bring over fruits and home-made cake . . . I thought she was coming to see me. And she would ask us to play tennis . . . Always at a time when she knew quite well I was busy. But I didn't see any harm in it. I was glad Conrad had a chance to relax. Because he worked very hard, and Delfzijl was a bit dull for him. Last year, she nearly came to Paris with us . . . and it was even my idea!'

She said all this simply, but with a weariness in which there was hardly any rancour.

'He can't have wanted to leave here . . . You heard . . . But he was afraid of causing pain to anyone. That was how he was. He used to be reprimanded for giving exam marks that were too generous. That's why my father didn't care for him.'

She put an ornament back in its place, and this precise housewifely act was at odds with the atmosphere in the room.

'I'd just like all this to be over. Because we're not even allowed to bury him. You know that? I don't know . . . I want them to give him back to me. God will see that the guilty one is punished.'

She became more animated. She went on, her voice firmer now:

'Yes! That's what I believe. Things like this, they're a matter between God and the murderer. What can we know?'

She gave a start, as if an idea had just struck her. Pointing to the door, she gasped:

'Perhaps he's going to kill her. He's capable of it. That would be terrible!'

Any was looking at her with some impatience. She must have been thinking all these words were of no help, and it was with a calm voice that she asked:

'So now, what do you think, *monsieur le commissaire*?'

'Nothing!'

She didn't insist. But her face showed her dissatisfaction.

'I don't think anything, because above all there is the matter of Oosting's cap!' he said. 'You heard Jean Duclos's theories. You've read the books by Grosz he told you about. One principle! Never allow yourself to be distracted from the truth by psychological considerations. Follow to the end the reasoning resulting from material evidence.'

It was impossible to know whether he was serious or whether he was teasing her.

'And here we have a cap, and the stub of a cigar! Somebody must have brought them or thrown them into the house.'

Madame Popinga sighed to herself:

'I can't believe that Oosting . . .'

Then suddenly, lifting her head:

'That makes me think of something I'd forgotten.'

Then she fell silent, as if fearing she had said too much, terrified by the consequences of her words.

'Tell me.'

'No, no, it's nothing.'

'I would still like . . .'

'When Conrad went seal-hunting on the Workum sand-banks . . .'

'Yes? What about it . . . ?'

'Beetje went with them. Because she goes hunting too . . . Here in Holland, girls have a lot of freedom.'

'Did they spend the night away?'

'Sometimes one night. Sometimes two.'

She took her head in her hands with a gesture of the most extreme frustration and groaned.

'No! I don't want to think about it! It's too horrible! Too horrible.'

This time, sobs were rising in her throat, ready to break out, and Any took her sister by the shoulders and gently propelled her into the next room.

7. Lunch at the Van Hasselt

When Maigret arrived back at the hotel, he realized that something unusual was happening. The previous day he had dined at the table next to Jean Duclos's.

Now, three places were laid on the round table in the centre of the dining room. A dazzling white cloth, with knife-sharp creases, had been spread. And at each place stood three glasses, which in Holland is only done for a truly ceremonial meal.

As soon as he came in, Maigret was greeted by Inspector Pijpekamp, who advanced towards him, hand outstretched, with the wide smile of a man who has arranged a pleasant surprise.

He was in his best clothes: a wing-collar eight centimetres high! A formal jacket. He was freshly shaved, and must have come straight from the barber's, for around him there still hovered a scent of Parma violets.

Less formally dressed, Jean Duclos stood behind him, looking slightly jaundiced.

'You must forgive me, my dear colleague. I should have warned you this morning . . . I would have liked to invite you back home, but I live in Groningen and I'm a bachelor. So I have taken the liberty of inviting you to lunch here. Just a simple lunch, no fuss.'

And looking, as he pronounced the last words, at the

cutlery and crystal glasses, he was obviously waiting for Maigret to contradict him.

He did no such thing.

'I thought that since the professor is your compatriot, you would be happy to . . .'

'Very good! Very good!' said Maigret. 'Would you excuse me while I go to wash my hands.'

He did so, looking grumpy, at the little washbasin in an adjacent room. The kitchen was next door, and he could hear much bustle, the clink of dishes and saucepans.

When he went back to the dining room, Pijpekamp himself was pouring port into the glasses and murmuring with a modest but delighted smile:

'Just like in France, eh? *Prosit!* Your very good health, my dear colleague.'

His goodwill was touching. He was making an effort to find the most sophisticated expressions and show that he was a man of the world to his fingertips.

'I ought to have invited you yesterday. But I was so . . . how would you say? So shaken about by this affair. Have you discovered anything?'

'No, nothing.'

The Dutchman's eyes lit up, and Maigret thought to himself:

'Aha, my little man, you've got some prize exhibit to show me, and you'll bring it out over dessert. If you have the patience to wait that long.'

He was not mistaken. The first course was tomato soup, which was served with a Saint-Émilion sweet enough to make you feel bilious, and obviously fortified for export.

'Your health!'

What a good show Pijpekamp was putting on! Doing his very best or even better. And Maigret didn't even seem to notice it. He showed no appreciation!

'In Holland, you know, we never drink with the meal, only afterwards. In the evening, on special occasions a little glass of wine with a cigar. And we don't have bread with the meal either.'

And he looked at the bread basket, which he had ordered specially. He had even arranged for port as an aperitif, instead of the national drink of genever.

What more could he have done? He was pink with excitement. He looked at the golden wine bottle with emotion. Jean Duclos was eating as if his mind were elsewhere.

And Pijpekamp had been so anxious to inject some gaiety into this lunch, to create an atmosphere of abandon, a real explosion of Frenchness!

The waiters brought in the national Dutch dish: the *hutspot*. The meat was swimming in litres of gravy, and Pijpekamp assumed a mysterious air to announce:

'Now, you must tell me if you like it.'

Unfortunately, Maigret was not in a good mood. He could indeed sense some kind of mystery in the air, but as yet was unable to fathom it.

It seemed to him that there was a kind of freemasonry between Duclos and the Dutch policeman. For instance, every time the latter refilled Maigret's glass, he stole a glance at the professor.

A bottle of Burgundy was warming by the stove.

'I thought you'd be drinking more wine.'

'That depends . . .'

Duclos was certainly ill at ease. He avoided joining in the conversation, and was drinking nothing but mineral water, claiming he was on a diet.

Pijpekamp could wait no longer. He'd chatted about the beauties of the harbour, the volume of traffic on the Ems, the University of Groningen, where the greatest scholars in the world came to give lectures.

'And now you know, we've come up with something new.'

'Really?'

'Your health! The health of the French police! Yes, now, the mystery is more or less cleared up.'

Maigret looked at him with his most neutral gaze, showing not the slightest trace of emotion, or even curiosity.

'This morning, at about ten o'clock, I was told that someone was waiting to see me in my office. Guess who?'

'Barens. Yes, go on.'

Pijpekamp was even more crestfallen than over the lack of effect the luxurious meal had had on his guest.

'How did you know? Someone told you, didn't they?'

'Not at all. What did he want?'

'You know him. Very timid, very – what's the French word? Reserved. He didn't dare look me in the eye. You'd have thought he was about to burst into tears. He confessed that on the night of the crime, when he left the Popingas' house, he didn't go straight back to the boat.'

At this point, the Dutch inspector gave a whole series of winks and nudges.

'You get it? He is in love with Beetje. And he was jealous because Beetje had been dancing with Popinga. And he was cross with her, because she'd drunk a cognac. He saw them both leave. He went after them at a distance. Then he followed his tutor back home.'

Maigret remained hard-hearted. And yet he could see that the other man would have given anything to receive some indication on his part of surprise, admiration or indeed discomfiture.

'Your good health, monsieur. Barens didn't tell us at first, because he was frightened. But now, here's the truth! He saw a man running away immediately after the gunshot, towards the timber yard where he must have been hiding.'

'And he described him in detail, I suppose?'

'Yes.'

The Dutchman was dripping with perspiration. He no longer had any hope of astonishing his colleague. His story was falling flat.

'A sailor. Undoubtedly a foreign sailor. Very tall, thin, clean shaven.'

'And naturally, a boat left early next morning.'

'Three have left since then. So it's obvious. The whole thing's as clear as day. It's not in Delfzijl that we should be looking. It was an outsider, no doubt some sailor who used to know Popinga in the past, when he was at sea. A sailor with a grudge, someone he'd punished when he was an officer or captain.'

Jean Duclos was obstinately presenting only his profile to Maigret's observation. Pijpekamp signalled to Madame Van Hasselt, who was sitting at the till in her Sunday best, to bring them another bottle. They still had the dessert to eat, a *pièce de résistance*, a cake decorated with three kinds of cream on which the name Delfzijl was written in chocolate icing.

Pijpekamp lowered his eyes modestly.

'Would you like to cut the first slice?'

'And you let Cornelius go?'

His neighbour started, and looked at Maigret as if wondering whether he had gone mad.

'But . . .'

'If it's all the same to you, we can question him together presently.'

'That will be quite easy. I can phone the college.'

'And while you're at it, you can telephone Oosting, and we'll question him after that.'

'Because of his cap? But now that's explained, isn't it? A passing sailor saw his cap on the deck. Picked it up and . . .'

'Naturally.'

Pijpekamp was close to tears. Maigret's grave yet hardly perceptible irony had unsettled him so much that he bumped into the door-frame of the café's telephone booth as he went to make his call.

Maigret remained alone for a moment with Jean Duclos, who was looking determinedly at his plate.

'You didn't ask him to slip me a few discreet florins perhaps, while you were about it?'

These words were spoken quietly, without bitterness, and Duclos raised his head, opening his mouth to protest.

'Hush. We haven't time to argue. You advised him to offer me a good lunch with plenty of wine. You said, in France that's the way to get round a public employee. Hush, not a word. And after that I'd be putty in his hands.'

'I swear . . .'

Maigret lit his pipe and turned towards Pijpekamp, who was coming back from the telephone, and who, as he looked at the table, stammered:

'You'll, er, accept a little brandy? There's some fine old stuff . . .'

'Please allow me to be the one offering the drinks now. Could you ask Madame to bring over a bottle of her best cognac and some brandy glasses?'

But Madame Van Hasselt brought them some shot glasses. Maigret got up and went over to the counter himself to fetch brandy glasses, which he filled to the brim.

'To the health of the Dutch police!' he said.

Pijpekamp did not dare protest. The alcohol brought tears to his eyes, it was so strong. But Maigret, with a ruthless smile, kept raising his glass and repeating:

'Good health to your police force! . . . What time will Barens be in your office?'

'In half an hour. A cigar?'

'Thank you, but I prefer my pipe.'

And Maigret refilled the glasses with such authority that neither Pijpekamp nor Duclos dared refuse to drink.

'What a beautiful day!' he said several times. 'Maybe I'm mistaken, but I have the feeling that tonight poor Popinga's murderer will be under arrest.'

'Unless he's sailing in the Baltic,' Pijpekamp replied.

'Bah! You really think he's that far away?'

Duclos looked up, the blood draining from his face.

'Is that an insinuation, inspector?' he asked sharply.

'What kind of insinuation?'

'You seem to be suggesting that if he is not far away, he might be very close at hand.'

'What a lively imagination you have, professor.'

They were within inches of an incident. Due in part, no doubt, to the glasses of cognac. Pijpekamp was scarlet in the face. His eyes were glistening.

As for Duclos, the effect of the alcohol was to make him deathly pale.

'Just one more glass, gentlemen, and we can go and interview this poor boy.'

The bottle was on the table. Every time Maigret poured out a glass, Madame Van Hasselt licked her pencil and noted each measure in her book.

As they stepped outside, hot sunshine and tranquillity engulfed them. Oosting's boat lay calmly at its berth. Pijpekamp clearly felt the need to hold himself straighter than usual.

They had only three hundred metres to walk. The streets were deserted. The shops stretched before them, empty of customers, but as clean and well stocked as if for an international exhibition about to open its gates.

'It will be well-nigh impossible to catch this sailor,' Pijpekamp declared. 'But it's a good thing we know it was him, because now we needn't suspect anyone else. I will write a report so that your compatriot, Monsieur Duclos, can be quite at liberty.'

He entered the local police station with far from steady steps, and bumped into a piece of furniture before sitting down rather too heavily.

He wasn't exactly drunk. But the alcohol had taken away

some of the mildness and politeness that characterize most Dutchmen.

With a rather expansive gesture, he tilted back his chair and pressed an electric bell. He spoke in Dutch to a uniformed policeman, who went out, returning a moment later with Cornelius.

Although Pijpekamp welcomed him with the utmost cordiality, the young man seemed to lose confidence as he entered the room, because his eyes had immediately lighted on Maigret.

'The chief inspector from Paris just wants to ask you about a few details,' Pijpekamp said in French.

Maigret was in no hurry. He sauntered across the office, puffing at his pipe.

'Well now, young Barens! What did the Baes say to you last night?'

The young man twisted his thin face in every direction, like a panicking bird.

'I . . . I think . . .'

'Come on, I'll help you. You still have your papa, don't you, out in the Indies? He would be very upset, wouldn't he, if anything were to happen to you? If you were to get into trouble? I'm guessing, but possibly perjury, in an affair like this, could land you several months in prison.'

Cornelius was choking, not daring to make a movement or to look at anyone.

'Come on, admit it, Oosting was waiting for you yesterday on the bank of the Amsterdiep, and he instructed you to tell the police what you in fact told them. Let's have the truth now: you never did see any tall, thin man hanging around the Popinga house.'

'I . . .'

But no. He didn't have the strength to resist. He burst into tears. He was in a state of collapse.

And Maigret looked first at Jean Duclos then at Pijpekamp with that heavy but impenetrable expression that made some people think him an idiot. Because that gaze was so neutral that it appeared completely vacant.

'So you think . . . ?' began the Dutch inspector.

'See for yourself.'

The young man, whose officer's uniform, by its formality, made him look even slighter than he was, blew his nose, and clenched his teeth to try and stifle his sobs, but finally stammered:

'I haven't done anything . . .'

They watched him for some moments, as he tried to regain control.

'That's all,' pronounced Maigret firmly at last. 'I didn't say you had done anything. Oosting asked you to claim you had seen a stranger lurking by the house. He probably told you that it was the only way to save a certain someone . . . Who?'

'I swear on the head of my mother he didn't tell me who. I don't know! I want to die!'

'Tut, tut! At eighteen, everyone wants to die. You don't have any more questions, Monsieur Pijpekamp?'

The Dutch officer shrugged his shoulders, a gesture signifying that he had no idea what was going on.

'All right, young man, you can be off now.'

'You know, it wasn't Beetje . . .'

'Possibly. Time for you to run off and join your college friends.'

And he pushed him outside, muttering:

'Next! Has Oosting arrived? Unfortunately that one doesn't understand French.'

The electric bell rang again. Presently, the duty officer brought in the Baes, who was holding his new cap as well as his pipe, which he had allowed to go out.

He looked in only one direction, at Maigret. And, strange to say, his expression was reproachful. He stood in front of the Dutch inspector's desk and greeted him.

'Would you mind asking him where he was when Popinga was shot?'

Pijpekamp translated. Oosting embarked on a long speech that Maigret couldn't understand, which didn't prevent him interrupting.

'No! Stop him. Just get him to answer the question in a couple of words.'

Pijpekamp translated. Another reproachful stare. And an answer, translated at once:

'On board his boat.'

'Tell him that is not true.'

And Maigret paced up and down again, hands behind his back.

'What does he say to that?'

'He swears it's true.'

'Right, well in that case, get him to tell you who stole his cap.'

Pijpekamp was all docility. It is true that Maigret was now conveying the impression that he was in charge.

'Well?'

'He was in his cabin. Doing the accounts. He saw through the porthole some legs up on deck. He recognized a seaman's trousers.'

'And he followed the man?'

Oosting hesitated, half-shut his eyes, snapped his fingers and spoke volubly.

'What's he saying?'

'That he prefers to tell the truth. That he is quite sure that his innocence will be recognized. By the time he got up on deck, the seaman was far away. He followed at a distance. And he was led along the Amsterdiep to a point near the Popinga house. Then the sailor hid. Oosting was intrigued, so he hid as well.'

'Did he hear the shot, an hour or two later?'

'Yes, but he couldn't catch the man who was running away.'

'He saw the man enter the house?'

'The garden, at any rate. He supposes he must have climbed to the first floor, using the drainpipe.'

Maigret smiled. The vague, contented smile of a man who is digesting his meal with total satisfaction.

'Would he recognize this man again?'

Translation, shrug of shoulders.

'He doesn't know.'

'He saw Barens spying on Beetje and his tutor?'

'Yes.'

'And since he was afraid he would be accused himself,

and since he also wanted to give the police a line to follow, he got Cornelius to testify on his behalf.'

'That's what he says. But I don't have to believe him, do I? He's clearly guilty . . .'

Jean Duclos was showing signs of impatience. Oosting was calm, a man who was now ready for anything. He spoke again and the policeman translated his words.

'He's saying now that we can do what we like with him, but that Popinga was both his friend and his benefactor.'

'And what are you going to do?'

'Hold him in custody. He's admitted he was there.'

Still under the influence of the cognac, Pijpekamp's voice was louder than usual, his gestures less controlled, and his decisions reflected this. He wanted to appear authoritative. He had a foreign colleague opposite him and he was trying to save his own reputation as well as that of Holland.

He assumed a serious expression and pressed the bell again. And when the duty officer hurried in, he gave orders punctuated by little taps of his paper-knife on the desk.

'Arrest this man! Take him away. I'll see to him later.'

All this in Dutch, but it was easy to understand what was being said.

Upon which, he stood up: 'I will try to clear this matter up for good. I shall of course report on the role you have played. And naturally your compatriot is free to leave.'

He did not suspect that Maigret, as he watched his Dutch colleague gesticulating wildly, his eyes bright with drink, was thinking to himself: 'My dear fellow, in a few hours' time, when you've calmed down, you will bitterly regret what you have done.'

Pijpekamp opened the door, but Maigret did not seem ready to leave.

'May I prevail on you for a final favour?' he said, with unaccustomed politeness.

'I am all ears, my dear colleague.'

'It's not yet four o'clock. Tonight we could hold a reconstruction of the drama, with all those who have been connected with it, closely or otherwise. Could you make a list of their names? Madame Popinga, Any, Monsieur Duclos, Barens, the Wienands, Beetje, Oosting and lastly Monsieur Liewens, Beetje's father.'

'You want to . . .'

'Re-enact the events, from the time the lecture ended at the Van Hasselt Hotel.'

There was a silence. Pijpekamp was thinking.

'I'll telephone Groningen,' he said at last, 'and ask my superiors for advice.'

He added, not quite sure how his joke would go down, and watching the faces of the others:

'But you know, someone will be missing. Conrad Popinga won't be able to . . .'

'. . . I will take his place,' Maigret finished the sentence.

And he went out followed by Jean Duclos, having issued his parting shot:

'And thank you for that excellent lunch!'

8. Two Young Women

Instead of going straight through town from the police station to the Van Hasselt, Maigret went round by the quayside, followed by Jean Duclos, whose bearing, expression, and the tilt of his head all indicated ill temper.

'You do realize you're making yourself utterly obnoxious?' he muttered at last, his eyes fixed on the crane unloading a ship in the harbour, as its arm swung across just above their heads.

'Because . . . ?'

Duclos shrugged, and walked on a few paces without replying.

'You wouldn't even understand. Or perhaps you're deliberately refusing to understand. You're like all the French . . .'

'But I thought we were the same nationality.'

'Yes, but I've travelled a lot. My culture is worldwide. I know how to fit in with the country where I find myself. But you, ever since you've been here, you've just been barging ahead without bothering about the consequences.'

'Without bothering to find out, for instance, whether people really want the murderer to be found?'

Duclos reacted angrily.

'Why should they? This wasn't a gangland killing. So the murderer isn't a professional criminal. We're not talking about someone who has to be put away in order to protect society.'

'So in that case . . . ?'

Maigret had a self-satisfied way of puffing at his pipe, with his hands behind his back.

'Just take a look,' Duclos said in an undertone, pointing to the scene all around them, the picture-book town, with everything in its place, like ornaments on the mantelpiece of a tidy housewife, the harbour too small for serious trouble, the placid inhabitants standing there in their yellow clogs.

Then he went on:

'Everyone here earns his living. Everyone's more or less content. And above all, everyone keeps his instincts under control, because that's the rule here, and a necessity if people want to live in society. Pijpekamp will confirm that burglaries are extremely rare. It's true that someone who steals a loaf of bread can expect a jail sentence of at least a few weeks. But where do you see any disorder? There are no prowlers. No beggars. This is a place of clean living and organization.'

'And I'm the bull in the china shop!'

'Hear me out! See the houses on the left, by the Amsterdiep? They're the residences of the city elders, wealthy men, powerful locally. Everyone knows them. There's the mayor, the church ministers, the teachers and civil servants, everyone who sees to it that nothing disturbs the peace of the town, that everyone knows his place and isn't a nuisance to his neighbours. These people, as I think I've already told you, don't even approve of one of their number going to a café, because it would be setting a bad example. Then a crime is committed. And *you* suspect some family quarrel.'

Maigret listened to all this as he watched the boats, their decks riding higher than the quayside now, like a series of brightly coloured walls, since it was high tide.

'I don't know what Pijpekamp thinks,' Duclos went on. 'Certainly he's well-respected. What I do know is that it would be preferable, and in everyone's interest, to announce this evening that Popinga's murderer was some foreign seaman, and that the search is still under way. For everyone's sake. Better for Madame Popinga. For her family. For her father, too, who's an eminent intellectual. For Beetje and *her* father. But above all for the sake of example! For all the people living in the little houses in this town, who watch what happens in the big houses on the Amsterdiep and are ready to do the same. But you, you want truth for truth's sake, for the glory of solving a difficult case.'

'Is that what Pijpekamp said to you this morning? And he took the opportunity, didn't he, to ask you how he could discourage my persistent habit of raising awkward questions? And you told him that in France, men like me can be bought off with a good lunch, or even a tip.'

'No such precise words passed our lips.'

'Do you know what I think, Monsieur Jean Duclos?'

Maigret had stopped, the better to admire the panorama. A tiny little boat, kitted out as a shop, was chugging along from ship to ship, barge to yacht trailing petrol fumes and selling bread, spices, tobacco, pipes and genever.

'I'm listening.'

'I think you were lucky to come out of the bathroom holding the revolver.'

'What do you mean?'

'Nothing. Just tell me, again, that you saw nobody in the bathroom.'

'That's right, I didn't see anybody.'

'And you didn't hear anything either?'

Duclos turned his head away.

'Nothing very clearly. Perhaps just a feeling that something moved under the lid of the bath.'

'Oh, excuse me – I see there's someone waiting for me.'

And Maigret strode off briskly towards the entrance of the Van Hasselt, where Beetje Liewens could be seen pacing up and down on the pavement, looking out for him.

She tried to smile at him, as she had before, but this time her smile was joyless. She seemed nervous. She went on glancing down the street, as if afraid of seeing someone appear.

'I've been waiting almost half an hour for you.'

'Will you come inside?'

'Not to the café, please.'

In the corridor, he hesitated for a second. He couldn't take her to his room either. He pushed open the door of the ballroom, a huge empty space where voices echoed as if in a church.

In broad daylight, the stage looked dusty and lacklustre. The piano was open. A bass drum stood in a corner and piles of chairs were stacked up to the ceiling.

Behind them hung paper chains, which must have been used for a dance.

Beetje looked as fresh-faced as before. She was wearing a blue jacket and skirt, and her bosom was more enticing than ever under a white silk blouse.

'So you were able to get out of the house?'

She did not reply at once. She obviously had plenty to say, but didn't know where to begin.

'I escaped!' she said at last. 'I couldn't stay there any more, I was scared. The maid came to tell me my father was furious, he was capable of killing me. Already he'd shut me in my room without a word. Because he never says anything when he's angry. The other night, we went home without saying a thing. He locked me in. This afternoon, the maid spoke to me through the keyhole. It seems he came back at midday, white in the face. He ate his lunch, then went stalking off around the farm. After that he visited my mother's grave. That's what he does every time he's going to make an important decision. So I broke a pane of glass in the door, and the maid passed me a screwdriver so that I could take off the lock. I don't want to go back. You don't know my father . . .'

'One question,' Maigret interrupted.

He was looking at the little handbag in glossy kid leather she was holding.

'How much money did you bring with you?'

'I don't know . . . Perhaps five hundred florins.'

'From your own bedroom?'

She reddened and stammered:

'It was in the desk. I wanted to go to the station. But there was a policeman on duty there, so I thought of you.'

They were standing there as if in a waiting room, where

an intimate atmosphere is impossible, and it occurred to neither of them to take two of the stacked chairs and sit down.

Beetje might be on edge, but she wasn't panicking. That was perhaps why Maigret was looking at her with some hostility, which found its way into his voice when he asked her:

'How many men have you already asked to run away with you?'

She was entirely taken aback. Turning away, she stammered:

'Wh— What did you say?'

'Well, you asked Popinga. Was he the first?'

'I don't understand.'

'I'm asking you if he was your first lover.'

A longish silence. Then:

'I didn't think you'd be so nasty to me. I came here . . .'

'Was he the first? All right, so it had been going on for a little over a year. But before that?'

'I . . . I had a bit of a flirtation with my gym teacher at high school in Groningen.'

'A flirtation?'

'It was him, he . . .'

'Right. You had a lover before Popinga, then. Any others?'

'Never,' she cried indignantly.

'And you've been Barens's mistress too, haven't you?'

'No, that's not true, I swear . . .'

'But you used to meet him . . .'

'Because he was in love with me. But he hardly dared even kiss me.'

'And the last time you had a rendezvous with him, the one that was interrupted when both I and your father turned up, you suggested running away together?'

'How did you know?'

He almost burst out laughing. Her naivety was incredible. She had regained some of her self-possession. In fact, she spoke of these delicate matters with remarkable frankness!

'But he didn't want to?'

'He was scared. He said he didn't have any money.'

'So you proposed to get some from your house. In short, you've been itching to run away for ages. Your main aim in life is to leave Delfzijl with a man, any man.'

'Not just any man,' she corrected him crossly. 'You're being horrible. You're not trying to understand.'

'Oh yes I am! A five-year-old could understand! You love life! You like men! You like all the pleasures the world has to offer.'

She lowered her eyes and fiddled with her handbag.

'You're bored stiff on your father's model farm. You want something else in life. You start at high school, when you're seventeen, with the gym teacher. But you can't persuade him to leave. In Delfzijl you look around at the available men, and you find one who looks more adventurous than the others. Popinga's travelled the world. He likes life too. And he too is chafing at the prejudices of the local people. You throw yourself at him.'

'Why do you say . . . ?'

'Maybe I'm exaggerating a little. Let's say, here you are, a pretty girl, devilishly attractive, and he starts to flirt a bit with you. But only timidly, because he's afraid of complications, he's afraid of his wife, of Any, of his principal and his pupils.'

'Especially Any!'

'We'll get to her later. So he snatches kisses in corners. I'm prepared to bet he wasn't even bold enough to ask for more. But you think you've hit the jackpot. You engineer meetings every day. You go round to his house with fruit. You're accepted into the household. You get him to see you home on his bike, and you stop behind the timber stacks. You write letters to him about your longing to run away . . .'

'You've read them?'

'Yes.'

'And you don't think it was him that started it?'

She was launched now.

'At first, he told me he was unhappy, Madame Popinga didn't understand him, all she thought about was what people would say, that he was leading a stupid life, and so on.'

'Naturally!'

'So you see . . .'

'Sixty per cent of married men say that kind of thing to the first attractive young woman they meet. Unfortunately for him, he'd come across a girl who took him at his word.'

'Oh you're so horrible, so horrible!'

She was on the point of crying. She restrained herself, and stamped her foot as she said 'horrible'.

'In short, he kept putting off this famous escape, and you started to think it was never going to happen.'

'That's not true!'

'Yes it is. As is proved by your taking out a kind of insurance policy against that happening, by letting young Barens pay his respects. Cautiously. Because he's a shy young man, well brought up, respectful, you have to be careful not to scare him off.'

'That's a mean thing to say!'

'It's merely what happens in real life.'

'You really hate me, don't you?'

'Me? Not at all.'

'You do hate me! But I'm so unhappy. I loved Conrad.'

'And Cornelius? And the gym teacher?'

This time she did shed tears. She stamped her foot again.

'I forbid you . . .'

'To say you didn't love any of them? Why not? You only loved them to the extent that they represented another life for you, the great escape you were always longing for.'

She wasn't listening any more. She wailed:

'I shouldn't have come, I thought . . .'

'That I would take you under my wing. But that's what I am doing. Only I don't consider you a victim in all this, or a heroine. Just a greedy little girl, a bit silly, a bit selfish, that's all. There are plenty of little girls like that around.'

She looked up with tearful eyes, in which some hope already glistened.

'But everyone hates me,' she moaned.

'Who do you mean by everyone?'

'Madame Popinga, for a start, because I'm not like her. She'd like me to be making clothes all day for South Sea islanders, or knitting socks for the poor. I know she's told the girls who work for those charities not to be like me. And she even said out loud that if I didn't find a husband soon, I'd come to a bad end. People told me.'

It was as if a breath of the slightly rancid air of the little town had reached them once more: the gossip, the girls from good families, sitting knitting under the watchful eye of a lady who dispensed good works, advice and sly remarks.

'But it's mostly Any.'

'Who hates you?'

'Yes. When I went round there, she'd usually leave the room and go upstairs. I'm sure she guessed the truth a long time ago. Madame Popinga, in spite of everything, means well. She just wanted me to change my ways, to wear different clothes. And she especially wanted to get me to read something different from novels! But she didn't suspect anything. She was the one who told Conrad to see me home.'

An amused smile floated across Maigret's face.

'But with Any, it's not the same. You've seen her, haven't you? She looks a fright! Her teeth are all crooked. She's never had a man interested in her. And she knows it. She knows she'll be an old maid all her life. That's why she did all that studying: she wanted to have a profession. She's even a member of those feminist leagues.'

Beetje was getting worked up. One sensed an ancient grievance coming to the surface.

'So she was always creeping around the house, keeping an eye on Conrad. Because she doesn't have any choice about being virtuous, she'd like everyone to be in the same boat. You understand? She guessed, I'm sure. She must have tried to get her brother-in-law to give me up. And even Cornelius! She could see that all the men look at me, and that includes Wienands, who's never dared say a word to me, but he goes red when I dance with him. And *his* wife hates me too, because of that. Maybe Any didn't say anything to her sister. But maybe she did. Maybe she's the one that found my letters.'

'And then went on to kill?' said Maigret sharply.

She stammered:

'N-no, I swear I don't know, I didn't say that. Just that Any's poisonous! Is it my fault if she's ugly?'

'And you're sure she's never had a lover?'

Ah, the little smile, or indeed giggle, in Beetje's answer, that instinctively victorious giggle of a desirable woman scorning one who is plain!

It was like little misses in boarding school, squabbling over a trifle.

'Not in Delfzijl, at any rate.'

'And as well as hating you, she didn't like her brother-in-law either, did she?'

'I don't know. That's not the same thing, he was family. And perhaps all the family belonged to her a little. So she had to keep an eye on him, see he didn't get into trouble . . .'

'But not shoot him?'

'What can you be thinking? You keep saying that.'

'I don't think anything. Just answer my questions. Was Oosting aware of your relationship with Popinga?'

'Did they tell you that too?'

'You went on his boat together to the Workum sand-banks. Did he leave you two . . . on your own?'

'Yes, he was up on deck, steering the boat.'

'And he let you have the cabin.'

'Naturally, it was cold outside.'

'You haven't seen him since . . . since Conrad's death?'

'No! I swear I haven't.'

'And he's never made any advances to you?'

She laughed out loud.

'Him?'

And yet she was again on the brink of weeping, clearly distressed. Madame Van Hasselt, having heard their raised voices, put her head round the door, then muttered her apologies and went back to her post behind the till. There was a silence.

'Do you really believe your father's capable of killing you?'

'Yes! He would . . .'

'So he might also have been capable of killing your lover.'

She opened her eyes wide with terror, and protested fiercely:

'No, no! That's not true! Papa wouldn't . . .'

'But when you got home on the night of the crime, he wasn't there.'

'How do you know that?'

'He came in a little later than you, didn't he?'

'Straight afterwards. But . . .'

'In your last letters, you showed signs of impatience. You felt Conrad was getting away from you, that the whole escapade was starting to frighten him, and that, in any case, he wouldn't leave his home to run off abroad with you.'

'What do you mean?'

'Nothing. Just recapping. Your father will soon be here looking for you.'

She looked around in anguish, and seemed to be searching for the exit.

'Don't be afraid. I will be needing you tonight.'

'Tonight?'

'Yes, we're going to stage a reconstruction of what everyone did the night of the crime.'

'He'll kill me!'

'Who?'

'My father.'

'I'll be there, never fear.'

'But . . .'

Jean Duclos came into the room, shutting the door behind him quickly and turning the key in the lock. He stepped forward, looking important.

'Watch out! The farmer's here. He . . .'

'Take her up to your room.'

'To my . . . !'

'Or mine, if you prefer.'

They could hear footsteps in the corridor. Near the stage was another door communicating with the service stairs. Duclos and Beetje went out that way. Maigret unlocked the main door, and found himself face to face with Farmer Liewens, who was looking past his shoulder.

'Beetje?'

The language barrier was between them again. They could not understand each other. Maigret merely interposed his large body to obstruct passage and gain time, while trying not to enrage the man in front of him.

Jean Duclos was quickly back downstairs, trying to look casual.

'Tell him he can have his daughter back tonight, and that he will also be needed for the reconstruction of the crime.'

'Do we have to . . .'

'Just translate, for God's sake, when I tell you.'

Duclos did so, in a placatory voice. The farmer stared at the two men.

'Tell him as well that tonight the murderer will be under lock and key.'

This too was translated. Then Maigret just had time to spring forward, knocking over Liewens, who had pulled out a revolver and was trying to press it to his own temple.

The struggle was brief. Maigret was so massive that his adversary was quickly immobilized and disarmed, while a stack of chairs they had collided with collapsed noisily, grazing the inspector's forehead.

'Lock the door!' Maigret shouted to Duclos. 'Don't let anyone in.'

And he stood up, recovering his breath.

9. The Reconstruction

The Wienands family arrived first, at seven thirty precisely. There were, at that moment, only three men waiting in the Van Hasselt ballroom, some distance apart, and not speaking to each other: Jean Duclos, on edge, pacing up and down the room, Farmer Liewens, looking withdrawn and sitting still on a chair, and Maigret, leaning against the piano, pipe between his teeth.

No one had thought to switch on all the lamps. A single large bulb, hanging very high up, cast a greyish light. The chairs were still stacked at the back of the room, except for one row, which Maigret had had lined up at the front.

On the little stage, otherwise empty, stood a table covered in green baize, and a single chair.

Monsieur and Madame Wienands were in their Sunday best. They had obeyed to the letter the instructions they had been given, since they had brought their two children with them. It was easy to guess that they had eaten their evening meal in haste, leaving their dining room uncleared, in order to arrive on time.

Wienands took his hat off as he walked in, looked around for someone to greet and, after thinking better of approaching the professor, shepherded his family into a corner where they waited in silence. His stiff collar was too large and his tie was awry.

Cornelius Barens arrived almost immediately afterwards, so pale and nervous that he looked as if he might run off at the slightest alarm. He also glanced around to see if he could attach himself to some group, but dared not approach anyone, and stood with his back against the stack of chairs.

Pijpekamp came in next, escorting Oosting, whose eyes lighted sternly on Maigret. Then came the last arrivals: Madame Popinga and Any, who walked in quickly, stopped for a second then both headed for the row of chairs.

'Bring Beetje down,' Maigret instructed the Dutch inspector, 'and have one of your men keep an eye on Liewens and Oosting. They weren't in here on the night of the murder. We'll only be needing them later. They can stand at the back for now.'

After Beetje arrived, looking flustered at first, then deliberately stiffening her back with an impulse of pride as she saw Any and Madame Popinga, there was a pause, while everyone seemed to hold their breath.

Not because the atmosphere was tense. Because it wasn't. It was merely sordid.

In that huge empty hall, with the single light bulb hanging from the ceiling, they looked like a random group of human beings.

It was hard to imagine that, a few days earlier, many people, the notable citizens of Delfzijl, had paid for the right to sit on those stacked chairs, had made their entrance hoping to impress others, exchanging smiles and handshakes, had sat down in their best clothes facing the stage and had applauded the arrival of Professor Jean Duclos.

It was as if the same sight were being viewed through the wrong end of a telescope.

Because of having to wait, and the uncertainty they all felt about what was going to happen, their faces expressed neither anxiety nor pain, but something else entirely. Empty, blank eyes, devoid of thought. Drawn features, giving nothing away.

The poor light made everyone look grey. Even Beetje did not seem alluring.

The spectacle was without prestige or dignity. It was pitiful or laughable.

Outside, a crowd had gathered, because the rumour had circulated in late afternoon that something was about to happen. But nobody had imagined it would be so lacking in excitement.

Maigret approached Madame Popinga first.

'Would you kindly sit in the same place as the other evening?' he asked her. At home, a few hours earlier, she had been a pathetic figure. But no longer. She had aged. Her poorly tailored suit made one shoulder look noticeably higher than the other, and she had large feet. And a scar on her neck, under her ear.

Any was in a worse case, her face had never seemed more lopsided than now. Her outfit was ridiculous, a scarecrow with a frumpish hat.

Madame Popinga sat down in the middle of the row of chairs, in the place of honour. The other evening, under the lamps, with all of Delfzijl sitting behind her, she must have been pink with pleasure and pride.

'Who was sitting next to you?'

'The principal of the Naval College.'

'And on the other side?'

'Monsieur Wienands.'

He was asked to come and sit down. He had kept his coat on, and sat down awkwardly, looking away.

'Madame Wienands?'

'At the end of the row, because of the children.'

'Beetje?'

She went to take her place unaided, leaving an empty chair between herself and Any: the one that had been occupied by Conrad Popinga.

Pijpekamp was standing to the side, unsettled, confused, ill at ease and anxious. Jean Duclos was awaiting his turn.

'Go up on the stage!' Maigret told him.

He was perhaps the person who had lost most prestige. He was just a thin man, inelegantly dressed. It was hard to think that a few nights earlier a hundred people had taken the trouble to attend his lecture.

The silence was as distressing as the light, at once revealing and inadequate, being shed from the high ceiling. At the back of the room, the Baes coughed four or five times, expressing the general feeling of disquiet.

Maigret himself did not look entirely at ease. He was surveying the scene he had set. His heavy gaze moved from one person to another, halting at small details, Beetje's posture, Any's over-long skirt, the poorly kept fingernails of Duclos, who was now all alone at the lecturer's table, trying to maintain his dignity.

'You spoke for how long?'

'Three quarters of an hour.'

'And you were reading your lecture from notes?'

'Certainly not! I've given it twenty times before. I never use notes these days.'

'So you were watching the audience.'

And Maigret went to sit for a moment between Beetje and Any. The chairs were quite close together and his knee touched Beetje's.

'What time did the event end?'

'A little before nine. Because first of all a girl played the piano.'

The piano was still open, with a Chopin Polonaise propped on the stand. Madame Popinga began to chew her handkerchief. Oosting shifted at the back. His feet were shuffling all the time on the sawdust-covered floor.

It was a few minutes after eight o'clock. Maigret stood up and paced around.

'Now, Monsieur Duclos, could you summarize for me the subject of your lecture?'

But Duclos was unable to speak. Or rather he seemed to want to recite his usual speech. After clearing his throat a few times, he murmured:

'I would not wish to insult the intelligence of the people of Delfzijl . . .'

'No, stop. You were talking about crime. What approach were you taking?'

'I was talking about criminal responsibility.'

'And your argument was . . . ?'

'That society is responsible for the sins committed within it, which we call crime. We have organized our lives for the good of all. We have created social classes, and every individual belongs in one of them . . .'

He was staring at the green baize table top as he spoke. His voice was indistinct.

'All right, that will do,' snapped Maigret. 'I know how it goes: "There are some exceptions, they're sick or they're misfits. They meet barriers they can't overcome. They're rejected on all sides, so they turn to a life of crime." That sort of thing, yes? Not original. With the conclusion: "We don't need more prisons, we need more rehabilitation centres, hospitals, clinics . . ."'

Duclos, looking sullen, did not reply.

'Right, so you were talking about this for three quarters of an hour, with a few striking examples. You quoted Lombroso, Freud and company.'

He looked at his watch, then spoke mainly to the row of chairs.

'I'm going to ask you to wait another few minutes.'

Just at that moment, one of the Wienands children started to cry, and her mother, in a state of nerves, gave the little girl a shake to quieten her. Wienands, seeing that this was having no effect, took the child on his knees and first patted her hand, then pinched her arm to make her stop.

The empty chair between Beetje and Any was the only reminder that what had happened was a tragedy. And even then it was hard to take it in. Was Beetje, with her fresh complexion but quite ordinary features, really worth breaking up a marriage for?

There was just one thing about her that was really

seductive, and it was the spell cast by Maigret's staging of the scene that had brought out that pure truth, reducing events to their crudest common denominator: her two splendid breasts, made even more enticing by the shiny silk surface. Eighteen-year-old breasts, quivering a little under her blouse, just enough to make them look even more luscious.

Along the row sat Madame Popinga, who even at the age of eighteen hadn't had breasts like that, Madame Popinga, swathed in too many clothes, layer upon layer of sober, tasteful garments, which took away from her any fleshly allure.

Then there was Any, skinny, ugly, flat-chested, but enigmatic.

Conrad Popinga had met Beetje: Popinga, a man who loved life, a man who had such an appetite for good things. And he hadn't been looking at Beetje's face, with her baby-blue eyes. Nor, above all, had he guessed at the desire to escape lurking beneath that china-doll face.

What he'd seen was that quivering bosom, that attractive young body bursting with health!

As for Madame Wienands, she was no longer a woman in that sense: she was all mother and housewife. Just now she was wiping the nose of her child, who had worn herself out with crying.

'Do I have to stay up here?' asked Duclos from the stage.

'If you please.'

And Maigret approached Pijpekamp, and spoke to him in an undertone. Shortly afterwards, the Dutch policeman went out, taking Oosting with him.

Men were playing billiards in the café. The clash of the billiard balls could be heard.

And in the hall, people's chests were constricted. It felt like a spiritualist session, as if they were waiting for some terrifying thing to happen. Any was the only one who dared stand up, abruptly, and after hesitating for a while she said:

'I don't see what you want us to do. It's . . .'

'It's time now. Excuse me, where is Barens?'

He'd forgotten about him. He located him, standing at the back of the hall, leaning against the wall.

'Why didn't you come and take your seat?'

'You said: the same as the other night . . .'

The boy's gaze shifted around, and his voice came out breathless.

'The other night I was in the cheap seats, with the other students.'

Maigret took no further notice of him. He went to open the door that led to an entry porch giving directly on to the street, making it possible to avoid going through the café. He could see only three or four silhouettes in the darkness outside.

'I presume that when the lecture finished, some people clustered around the foot of the stage: the college principal, the minister, a few elders of the town congratulating the lecturer.'

No one replied, but these few words were enough to conjure up the scene: the bulk of the audience moving towards the exit, the scraping of chairs, conversations and around the stage a little group: handshakes and words of praise for the professor.

As the room emptied, the last handful of people would finally move towards the door. Barens would come to join the Popingas.

'You can come down now, Monsieur Duclos.'

They all stood up. But everyone seemed unsure about the role he or she should play. They were watching Maigret. Any and Beetje were pretending not to see each other. Wienands, looking awkward and embarrassed, was carrying his younger child, a baby.

'Follow me.'

And just before they reached the door:

'We're going to walk to the house in the same order as on the evening of the lecture. Madame Popinga and Monsieur Duclos . . .'

They looked at each other, hesitated, then started to walk along the dark street.

'Mademoiselle Beetje! You were walking with Monsieur Popinga. So go along now, I'll catch up with you.'

She scarcely dared set off alone towards the town, and above all was afraid of her father, at present being guarded in a corner of the hall by a policeman.

'Now Monsieur and Madame Wienands . . .'

These two could behave the most naturally, since they had the children to look after.

'Now Mademoiselle Any and Barens.'

The last named almost burst into tears, but bit his lip and walked out past Maigret.

Then the inspector turned to the policeman guarding Liewens.

'On the evening of the murder, at this time, he was at

home. Can you take him there, and get him to do exactly what he did that night?'

It looked like a straggling funeral procession. The first to leave kept stopping and wondering whether they should keep going. There were hesitations and halts.

Madame Van Hasselt was watching the scene from her doorway, while exchanging remarks with the billiard players.

The town was three-quarters asleep, the shops all closed. Madame Popinga and Duclos headed straight for the quayside, the professor seemingly trying to reassure his companion.

Pools of light alternated with darkness, since the street lamps were far apart.

The black waters of the canal were visible, and boats bobbed gently, each with a lamp attached to its mast. Beetje, sensing Any following behind her, was trying to walk casually, but being on her own made that difficult to achieve.

A few paces separated each group. A hundred metres or so ahead, Oosting's boat could easily be seen, since it was the only one with a hull painted white. No light showed from the portholes. The quayside was deserted.

'Please stop where you are now!' Maigret called out, loudly enough to be heard by everyone.

They all froze. It was a dark night. The luminous beam of the lighthouse passed very high overhead, without illuminating anything.

Maigret spoke to Any:

'This is where you were in the procession?'

'Yes.'

'And what about you, Barens?'

'Yes, I think so.'

'You're sure? You were definitely walking along with Any?'

'Yes. Wait . . . Not here but a few metres further on, Any pointed to one of the children's coats, dragging in the mud.'

'And you ran ahead a little way to tell Wienands?'

'Madame Wienands, yes.'

'And that just took a few seconds?'

'Yes. The Wienands family went on, and I waited for Any to catch up.'

'And you didn't notice anything unusual?'

'No.'

'Go on another ten metres, everyone,' Maigret ordered. By that time, Madame Popinga's sister was level with Oosting's boat.

'Now Barens, go and catch up the Wienands family.'

And to Any:

'Pick up that cap from the deck!'

She had only to take three steps and lean across. The cap was clearly visible, black on white: the metallic badge on it was catching the light.

'Why do you want me to . . . ?'

'Just pick it up. '

The others could be glimpsed ahead of them turning round to see what was happening.

'But I didn't . . .'

'That doesn't matter. We haven't got enough people. Everyone will have to act several parts. It's just an experiment.'

She picked up the cap.

'Now hide it under your coat. And go and join Barens.'

Then he went on to the deck of the boat and called:

'Pijpekamp!'

'Ja!'

And the Dutch inspector showed himself at the forward hatch. It was where Oosting slept. There wasn't room for a man to stand upright inside it, so it made sense, if you were smoking the last pipe of an evening, say, to lean out and put your elbows on the deck.

Oosting was in precisely this attitude. From the bank, from the level where the cap had been placed, he could not be seen, but he would have been able to see the person who had stolen the cap quite clearly.

'Good. Now get him to act exactly the same as he did the other night.'

And Maigret strode on, overtaking some of the groups.

'Keep walking! I will take Popinga's place.'

He found himself alongside Beetje, with Madame Popinga and Duclos ahead of him, the Wienands family behind him, and Any and Barens bringing up the rear. There was a sound of steps further behind. Oosting, accompanied by Pijpekamp, had started to walk along the bank.

From that point, there was no more street lighting. After the harbour, one went past the lock, now deserted, separating the sea from the canal. Then came the towpath, with trees on the right, and half a kilometre ahead, the Popinga house.

Beetje stammered:

'I . . . I don't see what . . .'

'Hush. It's a quiet night. The others can hear us, just like we can hear the people in front of us and behind us. So Popinga was talking to you out loud about this and that, the lecture probably.'

'Yes.'

'But under your breath you were remonstrating with him.'

'How do you know?'

'Never mind. Wait. During the lecture, you were sitting next to him. You tried to press his hand. Did he push you away?'

'Y-yes,' she stammered, impressed, and looking at him wide-eyed.

'And you tried again.'

'Yes. He wasn't so cautious before, he even kissed me behind a door in his house. And once in the dining room, when Madame Popinga was in the parlour, and saying something to us. It was only recently he started to get scared.'

'So, you were arguing with him. You told him again that you wanted to go away somewhere with him, while you carried on the more innocent conversation in normal voices.'

They could hear the footsteps of the people ahead of them and behind, voices murmuring, and Duclos saying:

'. . . assure you that this does not correspond to any *proper* method of conducting a police investigation.'

And behind them Madame Wienands was telling her child in Dutch to behave herself. Ahead of them, the house loomed up through the darkness. There were no lights on. Madame Popinga stopped at the door.

'You stopped like this the other night too, didn't you, because your husband had the key?'

'Yes.'

The groups all caught up.

'Open the door,' said Maigret. 'Was the maid in bed then?'

'Yes, as she is tonight.'

After opening the door, she pressed an electric switch. The hall, with the bamboo coat-stand on the left, was now illuminated.

'And Popinga was in a good mood at this point?'

'Yes, very, but he was not his usual self. He was speaking too loudly.'

People took off their hats and coats.

'One moment. Did everyone take off their coats here?'

'Everyone except Any and me,' said Madame Popinga. 'We went up to our rooms to tidy ourselves up.'

'And you didn't go into any other room? Who put the light on in the parlour?'

'Conrad.'

'So please go upstairs.'

And he went up with them.

'Any didn't stay in your room, although she had to go through it to get to hers. Is that right?'

'Yes, I think so.'

'Would you be so good as to repeat exactly what you did? Mademoiselle Any, please go and put the cap with your hat and coat in your room. What did you do next, both of you?'

Madame Popinga's lower lip quivered.

'I . . . I just powdered my nose,' she said in a childlike voice. 'And combed my hair. But I can't . . . It's so awful. I seem to . . . I could hear Conrad's voice. He was talking about the wireless, and saying he wanted to listen to Radio-Paris.'

Madame Popinga threw her coat on the bed. She was weeping without tears, from nervous tension. Any, in the study which was her temporary bedroom, was standing still and waiting.

'And you came down together?'

'Yes. No. I can't remember. I think Any came down a little after me. I was thinking about getting the tea made.'

'So in that case, would you go downstairs now, please.'

He remained alone with Any, didn't say a word but took the cap from her, looked around and hid it under the divan.

'Come on.'

'How can you think . . . ?'

'No. Just come along. You didn't powder your nose?'

'No, never!'

There were shadows under her eyes. Maigret made her go down ahead of him. The stairs creaked. Below, there was absolute silence. So much so that when they entered the parlour, the atmosphere was surreal. The room looked like a waxworks museum. Nobody had dared sit down. Madame Wienands was the only one moving, as she tidied her older child's hair.

'Take your places as you did the other night. Where's the wireless?'

He found it himself, and switched it on. There was crackling at first, then some voices and strains of music, and finally he tuned it to a station playing a comedy sketch between two Frenchmen:

So this feller says to the captain . . .

The voice grew louder as the set was tuned. A few more crackles.

. . . And the captain, he's a good sort. But the other feller, nudge nudge, know what I mean? . . .

And this voice, that of a Parisian music-hall performer, echoed around the impeccable parlour, where everyone was standing absolutely still.

'Right, sit down, everyone,' Maigret thundered. 'Let's have some tea. Talk among yourselves.'

He went to look out of the window, but the shutters were closed. He opened the door and called:

'Pijpekamp!'

'Yes,' came a voice from the gloom.

'Is he there?'

'Yes, behind the second tree!'

Maigret came back inside. The door slammed.

The sketch was over and an announcer's voice said:

And now record number 2-8-6-7-5 from Odeon!

Some scratchy sounds. Then jazz music. Madame Popinga was huddled against the wall. Underneath the surface broadcast another voice could be heard, singing nasally in some foreign language, and sometimes there was a further spell of crackling before the music came through once more.

Maigret looked over at Beetje. She had collapsed into an armchair and was weeping bitterly. Through her sobs, she was whispering:

'Oh, poor Conrad, poor Conrad!'

And Barens, all the blood having drained from his face, was biting his lip.

'Tea!' Maigret ordered, looking at Any.

'We didn't bring it yet. They rolled back the carpet. Conrad was dancing.'

Beetje gave an even louder sob. Maigret looked at the carpet, the solid oak table with its lace cloth, the window and Madame Wienands, who didn't know what to do with her children.

10. Someone Waiting for the Right Moment

Maigret dominated them by his size, or rather his bulk. The room was small. Standing with his back to the door, he seemed too big for it. He looked serious. Perhaps he was never more human than when he said slowly, in a neutral voice:

'The music goes on playing. Barens helps Popinga to roll back the carpet. In a corner, Jean Duclos is talking to Madame Popinga and Any and listening to his own voice. Wienands and his wife are thinking it's time to leave because of the children, and are talking about doing so in low voices. Popinga has drunk a glass of brandy. That's enough to make him merry. He laughs. He hums the tune. He goes over to Beetje and asks her to dance.'

Madame Popinga was looking fixedly at the ceiling. Any's piercing eyes were directed at the inspector, who finished what he was saying:

'The murderer knows who is going to be the victim. Someone is watching Conrad dancing and knows that, in two hours, this man who's laughing a bit too loudly, who wants to be jolly in spite of everything, who is hungry for life and emotions, will be nothing more than a corpse.'

The shock made itself felt, literally. Madame Popinga's mouth opened to utter a cry that never came. Beetje was still sobbing.

The atmosphere had changed at a stroke. They might almost have been looking around expecting to see Conrad. Conrad dancing! Conrad, who was being watched by the eyes of the assassin!

Only Jean Duclos spoke, to say:

'That's a bit strong!'

And since no one was listening to him, he went on to himself, hoping Maigret might overhear him:

'Now I see your method, and it isn't original! Terrorize the suspect, suggest certain possibilities, place him in the context of the crime, to force a confession out of him. Sometimes when this is tried, the criminal repeats the same gestures in spite of himself.'

But it came across just as muffled muttering. Such words were hardly appropriate at a moment like this.

Music was still coming through the loudspeaker, and that was enough to lift the atmosphere a little.

Wienands, after his wife had whispered something in his ear, stood up timidly.

'Yes, yes! You can go,' Maigret told him, before he could say anything.

Poor Madame Wienands! A well-brought-up and most respectable citizen, who would have preferred to bid everyone goodbye politely, to get her children to do the same, but who didn't know how to manage it, and ended by shaking hands with Madame Popinga, without finding any of the right words!

There was a clock on the mantelpiece. The time it showed was five past ten.

'Not time for tea yet?' asked Maigret.

'Yes, it is!' Any replied, as she got up and went to the kitchen.

'Excuse me, madame. But didn't you go to make the tea with your sister?'

'A little later.'

'And you joined her in the kitchen?'

Madame Popinga passed her hand across her forehead. She was making an effort not to slump into stupor. She stared despairingly at the loudspeaker.

'I don't know. Wait a minute. I think Any came out of the dining room, because the sugar's kept in the sideboard there.'

'Was the light on?'

'No. Maybe. No, I think not.'

'And you didn't speak to each other?'

'Oh yes! I said: Conrad mustn't have any more to drink or he'll start misbehaving.'

Maigret went into the corridor, just as the Wienands were closing the front door. The kitchen was well lit and meticulously clean. Water was being heated on a gas cooker. Any was taking the top off a teapot.

'Don't bother actually making the tea.'

They were alone. Any looked him in the eye.

'Why did you make me take that cap?' she asked.

'Never mind. Come back in.'

In the parlour, nobody spoke or moved.

'Are you going to let this music go on playing for ever?' Jean Duclos managed nevertheless to protest.

'Perhaps. There's one more person I wish to see: the maid.'

Madame Popinga looked at Any, who answered: 'But she's in bed. She always goes to bed at nine.'

'No matter. Get her to come downstairs for a few minutes. She needn't bother getting dressed.'

And in the same flat voice he had used at first, he repeated obstinately:

'You were dancing with Conrad, Beetje. Over in the corner, other people were having a serious conversation. And someone knew there would be a death. Someone knew this was Conrad Popinga's last night on earth.'

The sound of steps was heard and a door banged on the second floor of the house, where the attic bedroom was. Then a murmur of voices. Any came in first. A shadow remained standing in the corridor.

'Come on,' said Maigret gruffly. 'Someone tell her not to be afraid to come in.'

The maid had indistinct features in a large plain face, and looked dazed. Over her cream flannelette ankle-length nightdress, she had simply thrown an overcoat. Her eyes were half-closed with sleep and her hair tousled. She smelled of her warm bed.

Maigret spoke to Duclos:

'Ask her, in Dutch of course, if she was Popinga's mistress.'

Madame Popinga turned her head away in pain. The sentence was translated.

The maid shook her head energetically.

'Repeat the question. Ask her whether her employer ever made any advances to her.'

More protestations.

'Tell her if she does not tell the truth, she risks a prison sentence. Divide the question up. Did he ever kiss her? Did he sometimes come into her bedroom when she was there?'

The girl standing there in her nightdress burst into tears, and cried out in her own language:

'I haven't done anything. I swear I haven't done anything wrong.'

Duclos translated. With pinched lips, Any was staring at the maid.

'Was she in fact his mistress, then?'

But the maid was unable to speak. She was protesting vehemently and crying. Asking to be forgiven. Her words were half drowned by her sobs.

'No, I don't think so,' the professor finally translated. 'From what I can gather, he did pester her. When they were alone in the house, he kept hanging around her in the kitchen. He kissed her. Once he came into her bedroom when she was getting dressed. He gave her chocolate in secret. But it didn't go any further.'

'She can go back to bed now.'

They heard the girl go back upstairs. A few minutes later, there was the sound of footsteps coming and going on the second floor. Maigret spoke to Any:

'Would you be good enough to go and see what she's doing?'

The answer was not long in coming.

'She wants to leave here at once. She's ashamed. She doesn't want to stay a minute longer in this house. She begs my sister's forgiveness. She says she'll go to Groningen or somewhere. But she won't stay in Delfzijl.'

And Any added aggressively: 'Is that what you wanted to achieve?'

The clock was now showing ten forty. A voice from the loudspeaker announced:

Our programme is over. Good night, ladies and gentlemen.

Then the sound of some other station's music came faintly through.

Maigret irritably switched the wireless off, and there was suddenly total silence. Beetje was no longer weeping, but was still hiding her face in her hands.

'And the conversations went on after that?' asked the inspector, with obvious weariness.

No one replied. Faces now looked even more drawn than in the Van Hasselt ballroom.

'Please accept my apologies for this painful evening.'

Maigret was speaking principally to Madame Popinga.

'. . . but don't forget that your husband was still alive. He was here, in rather high spirits because of the brandy. He probably drank some more . . .'

'Yes, he did.'

'He was a condemned man, you understand! Condemned by someone watching him. And others here, now, are refusing to say what they know, and are making themselves accomplices of the murderer.'

Barens gulped and started to shake.

'Aren't they, Cornelius?' said Maigret point-blank, looking him in the eyes.

'No! No! That's not true.'

'So why are you shaking?'

'I . . . I . . .'

He was about to have a panic attack, as he had on the way to the farm.

'Listen to me! It's about the time Beetje went off with Popinga. And *you* went out straight afterwards, Barens. You followed them for a while. And you saw something . . .'

'No. It's not true.'

'Wait. After the three of you had left, the only people in the house were Madame Popinga, Any and Professor Duclos. These three all went upstairs.'

Any nodded.

'And each of them went into his or her bedroom, yes? So tell me what you saw, Barens.'

He was casting about him desperately now. Maigret fixed the squirming boy with a look.

'No, no! Nothing.'

'You didn't see Oosting, hiding behind a tree?'

'No.'

'But all the same, you were hanging around the house. So you saw *something*.'

'I don't know, I don't want to . . . No, it's impossible.'

Everyone was looking at him. He dared not look at anyone. Maigret remained pitiless.

'It was on the road that you first noticed something. The two bikes had gone off together. They would have to pass through the place which is lit up by the lighthouse. You were jealous. You were waiting. And you had to wait a long time . . . A time that didn't correspond to the distance they had to cover.'

'Yes.'

'In other words, the couple stopped in the shelter of the timber stacks. That wasn't enough to frighten you. It would merely have made you angry, and perhaps despair of your chances. So you must have seen something else that frightened you. Something frightening enough, in any case, to make you stay put, although it was time for you to be back at college. You were between here and the timber yard. You could only see one of the windows of the house.'

At these words, Barens gave a start and lost control completely.

'You can't . . . You can't know that. I . . . I . . .'

'The window of Madame Popinga's bedroom. And there was someone at the window. Someone who, like you, had seen that the couple took far too long before they appeared in the beam of light from the lighthouse . . . Someone who knew therefore that Conrad and Beetje had stopped in the shadows for a long time . . .'

'It was me!' said Madame Popinga, in a clear voice.

Now it was Beetje's turn to react, and to stare at her, wide-eyed with terror.

Contrary to expectation, Maigret asked no further questions. Indeed, this created an atmosphere of unease. People in the room felt that having reached a culminating point, everything had stopped dead.

And the inspector went to open the front door, calling:

'Pijpekamp! Come here, please. Leave Oosting where he is. I imagine you have been able to see the lights going on and off in the Wienands house. They must be in bed.'

'Yes.'

'And Oosting?'

'Still behind the tree.'

The Groningen inspector looked around him in astonishment. Everything was very quiet. The faces were those of people who had spent night after night without sleeping.

'Would you stay here for a moment? I'm going to accompany Beetje Liewens outside, as Popinga did. Madame Popinga will go up to her room and so will Any and Professor Duclos. I would ask them just to do exactly what they did the other night.'

And turning to Beetje:

'Come along, please.'

It was cool outside. Maigret went round the building to the shed containing Popinga's bike and two women's bicycles.

'Take one of these.'

Then, as they rode calmly along the towpath towards the timber yard:

'Who suggested stopping?'

'Conrad.'

'He was still in a jolly mood?'

'No. As soon as we got outside, I saw that he was getting sad.'

They had reached the stacks of timber.

'Let's stop here. Was he in an amorous mood?'

'Yes and no. He was unhappy. I think it was because of the brandy, It cheered him up at first. He put his arms round me here. He said he was miserable, that I was a sweet little girl. Yes, those were his words, a sweet little girl, but I'd come along too late, and if we didn't take care, this would end in tears.'

'And the bikes?'

'We leaned them up here. I thought he was going to cry. I'd seen him like that before, when he'd had too much to drink. He said he was a man, so it wasn't so important for him, but a girl like me shouldn't throw away her life by having an affair. Then he swore that he was fond of me, but he didn't have the right to ruin my life, that Barens was a nice boy, and that I'd be happy with him at the end of the day.'

'And then?'

She breathed in deeply. Then she burst out:

'I shouted at him that he was a coward and I went to get on my bike.'

'What did he do?'

'He grabbed the handlebars. He tried to stop me. He said: "Let me explain . . . It's not because of me . . . It's . . ."'

'And what did he explain?'

'Nothing. Because I said if he didn't let go of me, I'd scream. He let me go. I pedalled off. He came after me, still talking . . . But I was going faster. All I could hear was him saying: "Beetje, Beetje, wait, listen!"'

'And that's all?'

'When he saw me reach the farm gate, he turned back. I looked behind me. I saw him bending over his bicycle, looking very sad.'

'And you ran back to him?'

'No! I hated him because he wanted me to marry Barens. He wanted a quiet life, didn't he? But then just as I was going in, I realized I didn't have my scarf. Someone might find it. So I went back to look for it. I didn't meet anyone. But by the time I finally got home, my father wasn't there. He came in later. He didn't say good night to me. He was looking pale and his eyes were angry. I thought he had been spying on us, and that perhaps he'd been hiding behind the timber stack. Next day, he must have searched my room. He found Conrad's letters, because I didn't see them after that. Then he shut me in.'

'Right. Come.'

'Where to?'

He didn't even reply, but cycled back to the Popinga house. There was a light in Madame Popinga's window, but she could not be seen.

'You think *she* did it?'

The inspector was muttering to himself:

'He came back this way, he was worried. He got off his bike, probably about here. He went round the house, wheeling the bike. He knew his peace of mind was threatened, but he was incapable of running away with his mistress.'

And then, suddenly:

'Stay here, Beetje.'

Maigret wheeled the bike along the path around the house. He went into the courtyard and towards the shed, where the varnished boat was a long silhouette.

Jean Duclos's window was lit up. The professor could be glimpsed sitting at a small table. Two metres along was the bathroom window, open, but in darkness.

'He probably wasn't in a hurry to go inside.' Maigret

was still talking to himself. 'He bent down to push the bike in under cover.'

Maigret fidgeted. He seemed to be waiting for something. And something did happen, but unexpectedly. A little noise up above, at the bathroom window, a metallic click – the sound of a revolver firing a blank.

And then immediately, there was the sound of a struggle, and of two bodies falling to the ground.

Maigret went into the house through the kitchen door, ran upstairs and into the bathroom, where he switched on the light.

Two shapes were wrestling on the floor: Pijpekamp and Barens, who was the first to give up, as his right hand opened and dropped the revolver.

11. *The Light in the Window*

'You idiot!'

Those were Maigret's first words, as he literally picked up Barens from the floor and held him upright, supporting him for a second, otherwise the young man would no doubt have fallen over again. Doors opened. Maigret thundered:

'Everyone downstairs!'

He was holding the revolver, handling it without precautions, since he had himself replaced its bullets with blank cartridges.

Pijpekamp was brushing down his dusty jacket with the back of his hand. Jean Duclos asked, pointing to Barens:

'Was it him?' The young naval cadet looked pitiful, not so much a hardened criminal, more a schoolboy caught out in some misdemeanour. He dared not meet anyone's eye, and didn't know what to do with his hands or where to look.

Maigret switched on the lights in the parlour. Any was the last to enter. Madame Popinga refused to sit down, and one sensed that under her dress her knees were trembling.

Then, for the first time, they saw the inspector looking awkward. He filled his pipe, lit it, let it go out, sat down in an armchair, but immediately stood up again.

'I have become involved in a case that has nothing to do

with me,' he began hurriedly. 'A French citizen was a suspect, and I was sent to shed light on the matter.'

He relit his pipe to give himself time to think. He turned to Pijpekamp.

'Beetje is outside, as are her father and Oosting. We must either tell them to go home, or to come inside. It depends. Do you want everyone to know the truth?'

The Dutch inspector went to the door. A few moments later, Beetje came in, timid and shamefaced, then Oosting with his obstinate expression, and finally Liewens, pale and wild-eyed.

Then they watched as Maigret opened the door into the dining room. They heard him feeling around in a cupboard. When he came back, he was holding a bottle of cognac and a glass.

He drank alone. His expression was grim. Everyone was standing around him and he seemed reluctant to speak.

'Do *you* want to know, Pijpekamp?'

And suddenly:

'Well, there's no help for it! No help for it, even if your method is the right one. We're different countries, different people. We have different climates. When *you* sense a family drama, you leap on the first bit of evidence that lets you explain away the crime. It must have been committed by some foreign seaman. That would be preferable perhaps, from the point of view of public morale. No scandal! No bad example being set by the bourgeoisie to the lower classes. Only *my* problem is I can still see Popinga, in this very room, turning on the wireless and dancing under the very eyes of his murderer.'

And he muttered crossly, without looking at anyone:

'The revolver was found in the bathroom. So the shot came from inside the house. Because it would be ridiculous to assume that the killer, after committing the crime, had the presence of mind to aim at a half-open window and throw the weapon inside. Let alone go and put a cap in the bath and a cigar in the dining room.'

He began pacing up and down, still avoiding looking anyone in the eye. Oosting and Liewens, neither of whom could understand what he was saying, were gazing at him intently, trying to guess what he was driving at.

'The cap, the cigar butt, and then the revolver taken from Popinga's own bedside table – it was all too much. Do you see? Someone wanted to provide too much evidence. To cause too much confusion. Oosting, or someone like him from outside, might have left half those clues, but not everything.

'Therefore, there was premeditation. Therefore, a desire to escape punishment.

'So we simply have to proceed by elimination. We can eliminate the Baes, first of all. What reason could he possibly have to go into the dining room and drop a cigar, then go up to the bedroom to look for the revolver, and finally to leave a cap in the bath?

'Next we can rule out Beetje, who in the course of the evening never once went upstairs, couldn't have left the cap, and couldn't even have taken it from the boat, because she was walking back from the lecture with Popinga.

'Her father could well have killed Popinga, after surprising him with his daughter. But by that stage, it was too late for him to gain access to the bathroom.

'Then there is Barens. He didn't go upstairs either. He didn't steal the cap. He was jealous of his tutor, but an hour beforehand, he had no certainty of what he suspected.'

Maigret stopped talking, and knocked out his pipe on his heel without worrying about the carpet.

'So that's all. It leaves us a choice between Madame Popinga, Any and Jean Duclos. There is no evidence against any of them. But it's not materially impossible for any of them to have done it either. Jean Duclos came out of the bathroom holding the revolver. We could take that as a sign of his innocence. Or it could be a very clever double bluff. But since he walked back from town with Madame Popinga, he couldn't have stolen the cap. And Madame Popinga, by the same token, being with him, couldn't have done it either.

'The cap could only have been taken by one of the last couple, Barens or Any. And just now, on the way here, I had it confirmed that Any remained alone for a moment or two alongside Oosting's boat.

'As for the cigar, let's not bother about it. Anyone could pick up an old cigar end anywhere.

'So, of all those who were here the night of the crime, Any is the only person who stayed upstairs without any witnesses, and who, we also know, had been into the dining room.

'But she had a cast-iron alibi concerning the crime.'

And Maigret, still avoiding looking at anyone, placed on the table the plan of the house drawn by Jean Duclos.

'Any could only have reached the bathroom by going

through either her sister's bedroom or that of the French visitor. A quarter of an hour before the murder, she was in her own room. How could she get into the bathroom? *And how could she be sure to be able to pass through one of the two bedrooms at the right moment?* Don't forget that she has not only studied the law but also forensic science. She's discussed them with Duclos. They talked together about the possibility of a crime which could be committed with mathematical impunity.'

Any, standing very upright and pale in the face, was nevertheless in control of herself.

'Now I will embark on a digression. I'm the only person here who didn't know Popinga. I have had to construct my idea of him from other people's evidence. He was keen to enjoy himself, but equally he was intimidated by his responsibilities and especially by received standards of proper behaviour. One day, in a jolly mood, he made advances to Beetje. And she became his mistress. Principally because *she* wanted it. I questioned the maid just now. And we know that he snatched kisses from her too, casually, in passing. But it didn't go any further, because he got no encouragement.

'In other words, he was a man attracted to all women. He was capable of taking small risks. A kiss in the corner, the odd caress. But above all, he was keen to ensure his own safety.

'He'd been an ocean-going captain. He'd known the delights of shore leave with no consequences. But he was also a servant of the Dutch Crown, and he wanted to hold on to his position, his house and his wife.

'He was a mixture of appetites and repression, imprudence and caution.

'Beetje, only eighteen years old, didn't understand that, and she believed he was ready to run away with her.

'Any lived in close proximity with him. Never mind that she is not particularly beautiful, she's a woman. A mystery therefore . . . and one day . . .'

The silence around him was painful.

'I'm not suggesting that he became her lover. But with Any, too, he was imprudent enough to make advances. She believed him. And she conceived a passion for him, though not as blind a passion as that of Madame Popinga. So here they were, all living together: Madame Popinga, suspecting nothing, Any more withdrawn, more passionate, more jealous and more subtle.

'She guessed he was having an affair with Beetje. She sensed the presence of the enemy. Maybe she even looked for the letters and found them.

'She could tolerate sharing him with her sister. But she couldn't accept this pretty girl brimming with good health who was talking of running away.

'She decided to kill.'

And Maigret concluded:

'That's all. Love that had turned to hate. Love-hate. A complex, wild emotion, capable of driving someone to any lengths. She decided to kill Conrad. Decided that in cold blood. To kill, without laying herself open to the least suspicion.

'And that very night the professor had spoken about crimes that were never detected, about unpunished murders.

'She is as proud of her intelligence as she is passionate. She committed the perfect crime. A crime that could easily be blamed on a prowler.

'The cap, the cigar and the unshakeable alibi: she couldn't escape from her room to fire the gun without going through either her sister's room or the Frenchman's. During the lecture, she saw the hands feeling for each other. On the way home, Popinga walked with Beetje. They drank, they danced and they went off together on their bikes.

'All she had to do was get Madame Popinga to stand for a while at her window, and insinuate something to make her suspicious of the pair who had just left.

'And while her sister thought she was in her own room, Any was able to creep behind her, already in her underclothes. Everything was planned. She got into the bathroom. She fired the shot. The lid of the bath was up. The cap was already in it. She just had to slip inside.

'On hearing the shot, Duclos rushed in, found the weapon on the window sill, and rushed out again, meeting Madame Popinga on the landing, and they went downstairs together.

'Any was ready and, half-undressed, she followed them. Who would ever suspect she wasn't coming straight from her room, in a state of panic? Here she was, appearing in public in her underwear, when she was known to be extremely prudish.

'No pity! No remorse! The hatred of a lover extinguishes any other feelings. There remains only the desire to conquer.

'Oosting, who had seen the person who took his cap, kept quiet. Both out of respect for the dead man, and from love of order. He didn't want scandal to surround Popinga's death. He even dictated to Barens what he should say to the police, so that they would just assume that this was a banal crime, committed by an unknown sailor.

'Liewens, who saw his daughter finally return home *after* Popinga had been accompanying her, and who next day read the letters, believed *Beetje* was guilty, so he locked her up and tried to find out the truth. When he thought I was going to arrest her earlier on, he tried to kill himself.

'And lastly we come to Barens. Barens suspected everyone. He was wrestling with the unknown and feeling under suspicion himself. Barens who had seen Madame Popinga at her window. Could it be that she had shot her husband, having discovered that he was unfaithful?

'Cornelius had been received here like a son. Orphaned of his own mother, he had found another in Madame Popinga.

'He wanted to devote himself to her. To save her. We forgot about him during the reconstruction. He fetched the revolver and went into the bathroom. *He wanted to shoot the only man who knew, and no doubt to kill himself afterwards.* A poor, heroic child. Generous as only an eighteen-year-old can be!

'And that's all . . . What time is the next train for France?'

Nobody said a word. They were all struck dumb with amazement, anguish, fear or horror. Finally Jean Duclos spoke:

'Well, a lot of good that has done . . .'

But Madame Popinga was leaving the room with mechanical steps and a few minutes later she was found on her bed, suffering a heart attack.

Any had not budged. Pijpekamp tried to get her to speak:

'Have you anything to say to this?'

'I will speak only in the presence of the examining magistrate.'

She was very pale. The deep circles under her eyes had spread to her cheeks.

Oosting alone remained calm, but he was looking at Maigret with eyes full of reproach.

And the fact is that at five o'clock in the morning, Detective Chief Inspector Maigret boarded a train, alone, at the little railway station of Delfzijl. No one had accompanied him. No one had thanked him. Not even Duclos, who had claimed he could only manage to catch the next train!

Day was breaking as the train crossed a bridge over a canal. Boats were waiting to pass, their sails flapping. An official was standing by to swing the bridge open after the train had gone across.

It was not until two years later, in Paris, that Maigret met Beetje again: she was the wife of a representative for Dutch electrical lamps, and had put on weight. She blushed when she recognized him.

She told him she now had two children, but gave him to understand that life with her husband was not up to expectations.

'And what about Any?' he asked her.

'Didn't you hear? It was all over the Dutch papers. She killed herself with a fork on the day of her trial, a few minutes before she was due in court.'

And she added:

'You must come and see us: 28 Avenue Victor Hugo. Don't leave it too late, we're off next week for winter sports in Switzerland.'

That day, when Maigret returned to headquarters, he contrived excuses to shout at all his inspectors.

OTHER TITLES IN THIS SERIES

And more to follow